Terrestrial Passions

by

S.P. Somtow

Diplodocus Press
Bangkok • Los Angeles

Terrestrial Passions

1

A Most Peculiar Frenchman

Tea-time in Little Chiswick changed little from one season to the next. Flanders House, its stateliest home, had been unoccupied since its Earl sought refuge from his gambling debts in the New World. Its other denizens of note, from the humblest drawing-room to the grand salon of Applethwaite Manor, sipped tea, launched conspiracies, and maligned their neighbours. Parsimonious or profligate, each tea-time was presided over by its particular matron, hell-bent on clambering to the loftiest position in the ton over the bloodied corpses of her rivals. Metaphorically, at any rate.

The widowed Mrs. Emma Dorrit, though possibly one of the least of these matrons, nevertheless entertained ambitions. Today, as most other days, she was simultaneously knitting, and bewailing the marital prospects of her twin daughters to her much put-upon brother, the vicar of St.

Stephen-of-Little-Chiswick, when a starship landed in her apple orchard.

That she did not notice it right away was not as surprising as it might seem; the appearance of such an object was so far beyond the perceptual world she had previously experienced that it were better for her sanity to ignore it. So, she assumed it was just some trick of the sunlight as it pierced the treetops and dappled the grass.

"My dear brother," she said, "surely getting the twins settled is a little more important than the text of Sunday's sermon."

Elsewhere in the orchard, her daughter Arabella was painting a watercolour, pausing now and then to admire her own handiwork. From this distance, Mrs. Dorrit could not identify the subject of the painting.

From inside the cottage, Anna, by five minutes the elder and by all accounts the stupider of the siblings, was essaying a nocturne by John Field on the pianoforte. At every wrong note, she let forth a vulgar utterance, one after another, most unseemly for a clergyman's niece.

The Reverend Lionel Bumbry, her brother, remarked: "Settling her would at least rid our household of that fearsome racket. I don't even know what half those words mean."

"Brother, you are too hard on her. She is an innocent, despite her impossible manners. Arabella, at least, has *some* accomplishments."

"Yet how you expect me to settle even one of your undistinguished offspring is a mystery," he continued. "You know very well that I have but forty pounds per annum. I am happy for you and your daughters, my very own flesh and blood, to dwell in this cottage, but beyond their board and lodging I can do little."

It was at that point that the starship landed, not ten yards from where the reverend and his sister were enjoying their tea. It was not a large vehicle; it fit quite snugly in a little clearing in the orchard. It was a gleaming, metallic thing with spikes, rotating gears, and coloured lights. For Mrs. Dorrit, it was simply indescribable, so she thought it best not to see it.

Mr. Bumbry did not even bother to look. Mrs. Dorrit was going to ask her brother whether he saw it, but thought better of it. After all, if she were seeing things, it wouldn't do at all for people to say that the penniless twins had a mad mother. In any case, Mr. Bumbry was fuming about something else. "Those confounded Catholics!" he exclaimed. "My sermon is going to demolish them for once and for all."

"Are you so suddenly moved to condemn the papists?" said Mrs. Dorrit.

"I am indeed," he responded. "For I have it on good authority that the Earl will be taking up residence in Flanders House again."

"Heavens!" said Mrs. Dorrit. "Catholics? Here?"

"It appears that the Earl has managed to pay off his debts by selling tobacco," he said.

"You mean to say … His Lordship has actually entered *trade?*" Mrs. Dorrit said, scandalized. "Those people have no shame!"

"The love of money is the root of all evil," said Mr. Bumbry. "Timothy 6:10 Although I daresay a belief in transubstantiation is the greater sin."

At that moment, a particularly noisome dissonance from within the cottage, followed by an ear-splitting "Oh, bugger!" caused Mrs. Dorrit to look up from her knitting. And it made it extremely difficult to ignore the entity that had now emerged from the starship and was standing right in front of her, hovering between the teapot and the clotted cream.

"If it please you," said the creature, "I require lodging for a few of your terrestrial revolutions."

"Answer the man," said Bumbry. "I'm not an innkeeper."

Mrs Dorrit said, "My dearest brother, I can barely lay eyes upon him, let alone address him. I bear no prejudice against his blue skin and pointed ears … surely some disease or deformity for which the gentleman cannot be at fault. But … he is completely naked!"

Indeed, he was. The creature stood tall and had the perfect musculature of an ancient Greek statue. His golden mane flew behind him as though animated by a powerful wind, though breeze there was none in the orchard of Applethwaite Manor.

"Naked?" said Mr. Bumbry, who had not yet looked up from his sermon. "He must be a foreigner. Pay the benighted thing no mind, my dear; some lost soul from the colonies, sans doute."

"If it please you," the stranger persisted, "I require lodging."

At length, Mr. Bumbry came to the rescue of his bewildered sister. "Sir, you have strayed into an apple orchard on the grounds of Applethwaite Manor, the estate of our distant cousin Lord Chuzzlewit, who has generously vouchsafed us this cottage to serve as the local vicarage as well as to house my sister and nieces. Perhaps if you ventured into the village, the innkeeper could address your needs. But you might want to clothe yourself."

Mrs. Dorrit hardly dared to confess even to herself that she found this creature's visage most striking. Indeed, there was a musky scent that emanated from his unclothed form that filled her with conflicting and most improper emotions. Furthermore, he possessed a kind of monstrous appendage, dangling from his nether region, which she could not help but stare at, for she had never seen such a thing before. She wondered, indeed, whether her husband had had such a ... but no, of course, he had been fully clothed, and with the lamps completely doused, on every occasion she had performed her wifely duty.

"It was hard enough," said the visitor, "to manufacture this terrestrial soma out of my adjustable protoplasm, so as not to cause too much panic at my advent. I am afraid the addition of clothing would require the expenditure of too much energy; I shall need to conserve it so that, once my vessel is repaired, I may return to my home planet."

"Just as I told you," said Mr. Bumbry to his sister, "he's not from these parts. But he is not a member of the darker races either, and despite his improper attire, he does have quite the civil tongue. But naked, indeed! Doubtless you have just come from some unholy, popish orgy in Flanders House! You're obviously a Frenchman!"

The foreigner paused, seeming to have trouble with the appellation "Frenchman". He tapped his left wrist a few times, as if trying to get some contraption to work. "Frenchman?" he said. "I suppose one could call it that."

"I would fetch my daughter Arabella from her painting,"

said Mrs. Dorrit, "as she counts your native tongue among her accomplishments. But I daren't allow her to gaze on a gentleman in your state of déshabillé."

"Be that as it may," said the visitor, "I require lodging. If you cannot provide it, please do me the honour of taking me to your leader."

"This is getting a little irritating, sir," said Mr. Bumbry. "I serve no man but God! Be off with you!"

At that point, the Frenchman (if that was what he was) placed five golden guineas on the table, one by one. He had no pockets. He seemed to be squeezing them out of the palm of his hand.

"Wait," Mrs. Dorrit said. "Dear brother, let us not be over-hasty." She picked up a coin and bit down on it; it definitely had the feel and texture of pure gold. "You did not steal this money. You … *made* it."

"Indeed, I have the ability to perform minor feats of transmutation, though the energy cost is somewhat prohibitive."

"Can you make more?" said Mrs. Dorrit.

"Madam, is five guineas not enough? I researched your world quite thoroughly before crash-landing here, and my onboard computer calculated the amount sufficient for a month's accommodation."

"So, you *can* produce more money … as and when you require it," Mrs. Dorrit said. "Why, sir, pray sit and have a cup of tea! I am sure that I can find some suitable clothing for you amongst my husband's old things."

"What!" said Mr. Bumbry. "You would admit this high priest of Mammon into our very home?"

"Our very home? Why, dear brother, this Frenchman has

singlehandedly settled the problem of your nieces' dowries! He shall have any room in the cottage he desires, and full board besides!"

Mr. Bumbry sighed.

"For I was an hungred, and ye gave me meat: I was thirsty, and ye gave me drink: I was a stranger, and ye took me in: naked, and ye clothed me," said Mrs. Dorrit, pressing her advantage. "Matthew, 25:35."

"I'm not entirely sure," said Mr. Bumbry, "that accepting payment in guineas is quite what Our Lord meant when he spoke of Christian charity."

"But, think, dear brother — you shall soon be rid of your nieces, both the foul-mouthed pianist and the bluestocking know-it-all! And no one shall know you have engaged in trade. I'm sure the Frenchman will not tell a soul." Mrs. Dorrit stole another glance at the foreigner's impressive fleshy engine. "Come, I shall get you some clothes. I don't want another woman laying eyes on … that thing."

2

Universally Acknowledged

Miss Arabella Dorrit would not be formally admitted into the presence of the stranger until, as her mother put it, certain "standards of decency" had been put in place. She realized this and waited patiently

But of course, she had observed the entire meeting, as her easel had been set a scant thirty yards away from the tea-table. However, it would not have been at all proper for her to address the stranger without an introduction.

However, as soon as her mother and uncle had quit the orchard in order to attend to the visitor's attire, Arabella found herself alone in the orchard. Faintly accompanied by her sister's wrong notes and curses, she examined the vessel which had just landed.

It was of an iridescent, metallic lustre she had never seen. It was larger than a four-horse carriage, but not by much. Its only entrance was a round portal which had a rather indelicate pucker. There were what looked like portholes, from which a pale blue light emanated. The vehicle emitted a low, musical thrum which had the odd effect of blending with, and softening, the painful dissonances that issued from within the cottage. For the first time, Arabella found her sister's pianoforte performance to be almost … beautiful.

She went to the open window, where she could see her sister Anna labouring mightily at the pianoforte. "Anna, my dear," she whispered, "there's something you simply must see."

Pausing from her nocturne for a moment, Miss Anna said, "Unless I can play this nocturne from beginning to end, I'll never be able to perform at Lord Chuzzlewit's next soirée."

"We haven't been invited," Miss Arabella reminded her.

Sulkily, Miss Anna closed the lid of the pianoforte and came out into the orchard. She seemed remarkably uninterested in the contraption as her sister examined it admiringly. "You know as well as I do," she said, "that I simply don't care for the French. All these gaudy coloured lights! All these rainbow-metal curlicues and ornaments! A sober English coach-and-four, in basic black, would be far less vulgar."

"My dear Anna, there is nothing French about this contraption. How can you presume to judge?"

"But Mama said that the visitor was a Frenchman. I'm already feeling rather queasy about the impending introduction."

"How would Mama know? She has never been to Surrey, let alone to France! No, sister — it is my belief that this visitor is more than a foreigner. I am convinced he comes from another world entirely."

"And *you* would know such a thing? Why, dear sister, you haven't been to Surrey either."

"Yet I do know that Surrey is not unlike our own West London."

Arabella was used to her sister's insouciance, believing it to be a sort of self-defence for concealing her ignorance of the world. Combined with her lack of accomplishments, it did not make her terribly desirable in the marriage market; and yet, Arabella reflected, her sister's devil-may-care attitude might have been deemed charming in a woman of means. "I know you are anxious to get back to your nocturnes," she said, "but consider this: what if this visitor were not from France, but from another planet?"

"Absurd, my dear sister."

"Why, our great astronomer, Mr. Herschel, as gone so far as to say that *the stars are suns, and suns are inhabitable…we may have an idea of numberless globes that serve for the inhabitation of living creatures.*" She remembered this quote perfectly because she had just been spending an afternoon in Lord Chuzzlewit's library; that massive room contained almost every tome known to man, though his Lordship was more concerned that the volumes be uniformly bound than with actually reading any of them. She had taken the liberty of borrowing the book, knowing that her cousin would never notice.

"Mr. Herschel! But he's German," her sister said disdainfully.

"And he is also the Astronomer Royal … to our *German* king!" Arabella knew that Mr. Herschel had actually discovered another world. He had tried to name it "George," but the classical scholars won the argument with the much more pedestrian "Uranus." But she decided that to regale Miss Anna with more scientific trivia would inevitably bring more comments about bluestockings.

"Ah, sister, you and I ... so alike in looks ... so alike in our lack of a dowry. And yet there is one thing that differentiates us; for though he made us identical twins, God saw fit to grant only one brain between the two of us, and to house it in *your* skull almost entire."

For Anna did not resent being stupid — Arabella would have found that most distressing — indeed, she believed that Anna was far happier than she for not being burdened with the constant desire to apprehend and comprehend the world at large.

Their repartee was interrupted by a summons from inside the cottage. It was time for a proper introduction to the visitor ... Frenchman or otherwise.

Upon entering the drawing-room, Arabella was a little nonplussed to see the stranger seated in her father's armchair — which Mrs. Dorrit generally insisted should *not* be sat in — and wearing her father's knee-length tails with some ill-fitting pantaloons. Despite the blue skin and pointed ears, he was an imposing figure. Arabella's uncle stood stiffly behind the armchair, and her mama was chattering very quickly, as she frequently did when nervous.

"Ah, there you are, my dears," she said. "I'd like to introduce you to ... well, I cannot quite pronounce such a barbarous name, but it is something like Monsieur Clatoux. He will be living in the guest room for a time, as he needs to be able to repair his, ah —"

"Starship," said Clatoux.

"Monsieur," said Mrs. Dorrit, "my daughter Arabella speaks French quite well. Well, go on, dear, show him!"

Arabella curtsied and said, "Enchantée, cher monsieur, d'avoir fait votre connaissance."

As she well knew would happen, the visitor looked decidedly perplexed. He fiddled with his wrist for a second, then responded, "*Sehr angenehm, gnädiges Fräulein. Sie ist aber reizend, mich dünkt.*"

What kind of game was this? Arabella had of course studied German — one never knew when one might be summoned to Court one day — and so was able to answer in the same language, "*Doch keineswegs so reizend wie Er, mein gütiger Herr.*"

He touched his wrist again and responded: "Da, da, tovarishch." And Arabella *knew* he was not of this earth. For the movement of his lips was not perfectly synchronized with the words that issued therefrom. There was some kind of translating device concealed within his wrist. His real language was probably not any sort of human language whatsoever. *How thrilling*, she thought! *That I, a penniless girl from Little Chiswick, should be the chosen vessel for first contact between humans and the extraterrestrial beings described by the Astronomer Royal!*

"I see," said Mrs. Dorrit, "that you have already made some inroads in communicating with my daughter Arabella. I am so happy we made her learn French, though I must emphasize that there are no papists in this house."

"Our guest will be your responsibility, Arabella," said Mr. Bumbry. "We shall rely on your to show him the village, and to instruct him in the ways of the ton should that become necessary, and to rein him in should he display any outlandish French behaviour."

"But," Arabella said, "I couldn't possibly be seen with a man alone … especially a foreigner."

"We shall make sure you are adequately chaperoned, of course," said Mrs. Dorrit. "And now, I want you all to be properly seated, as I have matters of great import to announce."

Arabella and her sister found seats — Arabella on the divan, Anna on the pianoforte stool. Mrs. Dorrit rang a little bell, and the household servants — numbering only three since Mr. Dorrit's demise and the family's consequent descent into genteel poverty — stood in the back — being Mrs. O'Keefe, the cook, Pauline, the maid-of-all-work, and Japheth, an African who had once been a favoured page to the dowager Lady Chuzzlewit. Japheth had come down in the world since outgrowing his childhood, for there is little charm in a grown African in a powdered wig scurrying to fetch and carry for a noblewoman. The Dorrits' three servants were part of Lord Chuzzlewit's bounty; he did not want it said that his relations could not afford help.

Monsieur Clatoux surveyed this motley assemblage with interest, noting, Arabella was sure, the exact placement of each person in the room and thereby in the hierarchy of society. *Why,* she thought, *he is studying us, almost as though we were biological specimens in a scientist's laboratory! How exciting!*

"First," Mrs. Dorrit announced, "Monsieur Clatoux is to be catered to in every possible way, his every wish granted — within the limitations of decency, at any rate! — Mrs. O'Keefe, do find out what he likes to eat. If we must have frog pie one evening, let our guest not be denied! Anna, you shall practise the pianoforte *only* when Monsieur is out of earshot. Pauline, the second best sheets — on second thought, the *best*. Japheth, you shall serve as Monsieur's personal dogsbody, fetching and carrying whatever he wishes — for he assures me that your bloated proportions are of no import to him. The reason for all this is very simple. Monsieur Clatoux has a seemingly unlimited supply of gold. We shall have dowries. Our girls shall be settled with fine gentlemen of means. And I, mark you, *I* will finally be a woman of importance in the ton."

Arabella said, in wonderment, "And the monsieur has agreed to all this?"

"Indeed I have," said Monsieur.

"I have pressed upon Monsieur Clatoux," said Mrs. Dorrit, "that these goals ... the advancement of my daughters ... my own prospective elevation to a position of influence and power ... are crucial to his being able to remain here long enough to accomplish the necessary repairs to his carriage."

"It seems," Arabella said, "that the marriage game is understood in every nation. Is that not so, Monsieur?"

"Well ... it is of some interest for me to study your mating rituals," he responded. "On my world, there are seven genders, all of which need to come to an understanding in order to reproduce the race, so the game is infinitely more labyrinthine. Your simplistic society provides a fascinating view of a profoundly complex subject. Just two sexes! Such a bifurcation is a rarity among organisms. Such purity! Such primal primitivity! I only regret that by inserting myself into these observations, I may somehow distort the data."

"My word," said Mrs. Dorrit. "The customs of the French are inscrutable, to be sure."

"Yet passion, and property, and the propagation of the species," said Monsieur, "are significant motivations that motivate the lives of all races."

"Indeed," said Arabella, "considering the immense distance from which you have travelled, I would venture to call these truths *universally* acknowledged."

3

Dissuasion

The next few days passed with nary an interruption for the Dorrits. Mrs. Dorrit whiled away the hours with strategy sessions, listing the notable bachelors in the bon ton in order of desirability, with their position in the peerage, if any, their income per annum, and other distinguishing features. Monsieur Clatoux sat with her often as she mused. She had each prospect's name written on a small piece of card, the better to rank them.

At times, such as upon this Saturday afternoon, they sat in the orchard, where Anna's assault on the pianoforte was less painful to the ears. Arabella, meanwhile, would paint, or study her books, or practice her languages all by herself.

"I wonder that you do not ask your daughters' opinion on these matches," said Monsieur, sipping his third cup of tea.

"Why?" Mrs. Dorrit said. "Arabella is far too astute to

favour any man, and my poor Anna has no opinions at all. She is the perfect illustration of a seed thrown on stony ground. And I despair of Arabella, for no man likes to believe a woman his intellectual superior, this, despite the fact that we women run the world."

"Yes. In my study of your race, I have noticed that behind every successful male, there seems to be a thoughtful, conniving, secretive, manipulating female."

"You understand us well, then," said Mrs. Dorrit. "I had not thought the French so perceptive." She realized that she was becoming quite fond of Monsieur. She missed having Mr. Dorrit to tease. She had already figured out that Monsieur was not French, but it was a convenient fiction, and it meant she did not have to venture too far outside her familiar view of the universe. "But back to the list … Monsieur Clatoux, what do you think of Mr Higginbotham?"

"I wonder rather, Mrs. Dorrit, why the Earl is not amongst your chosen ones. He has taken up residence in Flanders House after a lengthy absence, has an immense fortune from tobacco estates in Virginia, and is accounted handsome by men and women alike."

"Heavens, Monsieur! How little you understand! The Earl is a Catholic."

"Heavens indeed!" Monsieur remarked, though Mrs. Dorrit noted that he betrayed more bewilderment than outrage.

"You shall comprehend all, Monsieur, when you go to church with us tomorrow. For, regardless of your beliefs, it would not do to have our house guest not appear in church. The ton must have something to gossip about, after all, and my brother has prepared a fiery sermon that will explain in precise detail just how un-English these papists are."

Miss Arabella was glad of an opportunity to walk alongside Monsieur Clatoux on the way to church. Her mother, sister, Mr. Bumbry, and Japheth the footman had already gone ahead, as Arabella's uncle had much preparation to undertake.

It was a short distance, only about three-quarters of a mile. But one had to pass a narrow strip of land that led to a rear entry to Flanders House.

"In the past," Arabella explained, "the Earl's estate did not border on this road at all. But the Earl's grandfather purchased a small strip of land from my cousin's grandfather, enabling his servants to reach the main village quickly instead of having to take the long way round. It was in the name of tolerance, since we no longer persecute Catholics in this country."

"And whom," Monsieur inquired abruptly, "would *you* prefer to marry?"

"Why, Monsieur Clatoux! You make me blush."

"I have noticed that your mother does not consider your opinion to carry much weight in the matter."

"She assumes I shall marry whomever she commands. Whereas I am sure I shall only marry for love."

"Your mother doesn't even believe such marriages are possible. She thinks that only flighty young maidens believe so, and that you, being exceptionally levelheaded, would be immune to such fantasies."

Arabella laughed. How little her mother understood the

complexities of her nature! For her intellectual pursuits concealed a far profounder sensibility. It seemed that only this being from another world had any real understanding of her at all.

A gentleman on horseback rode past them in the opposite direction and when she stopped to look for a moment, she saw him turn down the pathway to Flanders House.

"I am most grateful to be walking with you," she said, "and that Mrs. O'Keefe, my putative chaperone, is a hundred paces behind us, and will only be spurred to action if you should do something truly untoward, such as touching my elbow."

"Ah, Mrs. O'Keefe. I chanced to converse with her in the kitchen. She told me that *she* is a Catholic, yet she serves in your very house. Surely that is a little … dare I say it … hypocritical?"

"That may well be, but after all she is only an Irishwoman. One cannot expect too much, and besides, she is happy to go to our church and put on a show of devotion. What she will do later, for she has Sunday afternoons off, we take pains not to enquire too deeply."

But now the charming Saxon church of St. Stephen-of-Little-Chiswick loomed ahead. It was time for all to be on display, as much as they could be. Arabella entered the vestibule and showed Monsieur where the family's assigned seats were; not far from the front, as befit the family of the vicar, yet not at the very front, since there were many people of standing to be accommodated, including their cousins from the manor, and other landed gentry of varying degrees.

The Dorrits had a fair distance to process up the aisle,

and Arabella could not help but notice the titters. She even turned to scold some child who rudely commented on Monsieur's skin colour. "An inherited illness," she said. "Pray do not mention it to him; it pains him greatly to think on it." The child's mother immediately turned to her neighbour and passed on the gossip. Within the hour, Arabella knew, there would be no more public talk about Monsieur Clatoux's distinctive coloration. Although doubtless the whispers would increase.

Anna, who cared not a fig for public appearances, had already sat down, in the wrong place, next to some of her friends. Miss Arabella explained to Monsieur that there was no compulsory seating in this holy place, merely the requirements of custom, which were flouted at the peril of one's social standing.

Mrs. O'Keefe and Japheth remained in the vestibule, the former because she belonged to the other persuasion, the latter because of his condition of servitude, though an exception would undoubtedly have been made were he still the darling, costumed little black page who once attended Arabella's late cousin. Only the maid had remained at home, for it would not do to leave the cottage completely unattended. She had already been to church at six in the morning.

Mr. Bumbry celebrated the service with his customary grace, cutting a fine figure in his vestments. Monsieur watched with interest what he called "your metaphorical cannibalistic ritual," and when Arabella's uncle came to deliver the sermon, he took everything in with interest, pausing to ask Arabella the odd question ... and in some instances, the *very* odd question.

"Today I begin not with scripture," Mr. Bumbry began, "but with this invitation to a ball ... at Flanders House! How many of you have received such a missive from the newly returned occupant of that manse? How many have accepted this invitation from the hand of Satan himself?"

Titters ran round the congregation and indeed, several copies of the aforementioned epistle were pulled out of bosoms and pouches. It was to be noted, however, that Miss Arabella herself had not seen it before. Doubtless it had arrived at the cottage and been immediately seized upon by Mr. Bumbry; or — the horror — it had only come to Applethwaite itself, with the vicar's cottage being deemed too insignificant for something of such import. Neither alternative would please my mother, Miss Arabella reflected.

"Let me therefore, dearly beloved, remind you that the Earl's family has been in disgrace for some three centuries, having fled to France rather than give up its beliefs in such superstitions as *transubstantiation,* which modern science holds to be a figment of the imagination...."

Monsieur whispered in Arabella's ear. "What, I pray, is transubstantiation?"

She responded, "It is the literal transformation of bread into the flesh of Our Lord by magical means."

He said, "What is so unscientific about that? Where do you think *my* flesh comes from? Do you think we really look like this, on our own world?"

The revelation gave Arabella pause. "And the golden guineas?" she said.

"Programmable protoplasm. I am giving your family of my personal bodily substance," he said, "that your mother may rise in status, and that you and your sister may be properly settled."

What a positively Christlike sacrifice! Arabella thought.

"What irks me, rather," whispered Monsieur Clatoux, "is that so much energy would be expended on a petty so-called miracle, when it could profitably be used for the betterment of your species."

Mr. Bumbry continued his tirade. "Yes, it is true that the Earldom has been in existence since the time of William the Conqueror, and even predates our own Hanoverian dynasty ... and that when the family returned to Flanders House their titles and precedence were not taken away. Yet ... they are not quite ... like us. There is a popish chapel on their very grounds. There, they practise foul rites, swathed in incense, and deifying our Blessed Virgin Mary! They worship peculiar bones and even foreskins, imbuing them with supernatural powers!"

"Mr Bumbry forgets," said Arabella, "that a relic of St. Stephen is buried in the very altar where he just celebrated communion!"

Her uncle went on: "Why, their clergy may not even marry! I have no doubt that their seminaries are hotbeds of corruption, veritable Sodoms and Gomorrahs!"

"But Mr. Bumbry himself is not married," Monsieur whispered.

"My uncle is firmly wedded to his work," said Arabella, "and besides, his modest annuity renders him attractive only to women beneath his station."

Several prim ladies turned to shush her. 'My uncle's fire-and-brimstone attitudes," she whispered, "are a little too severe for modern folk."

"At any rate," Mr. Bumbry continued, "it is not my place to forbid any in this ton from attending the Earl's ball, which will have become, by default, the opening event in the coming season. It is for just such temptations that our good Lord gave the human race free will. But I must warn you all —" He raised his bible high above his head, and continued it a voice so thunderous it could well have been the Almighty in person — "if any of you return from this ball, and begin crossing yourselves, genuflecting, babbling in Latin, flaunting rosaries, or demanding extreme unction on your deathbeds, this congregation will take it most ill!"

Well! Arabella was used to such fiery speeches from her uncle, but at least he had not outright forbidden his congregation from attending such a ball — which would undoubtedly be the most exciting, and most scandal-worthy, of the entire season.

Once the service ended, the Dorrits were the subject of some attention, and Mrs. Dorrit was delighted to show off her house guest — indeed, she was positively preening. Mr. Bumbry remained behind with Japheth in order to finish his farewells to the congregation and supervise the cleaning of the church. Indeed, the Oglethorpes, who normally never even spoke to Arabella's mama, offered to take her and her guest in their carriage back to Applethwaite—the better, she supposed, to learn more of Monsieur and his mysterious congenital disease, not to inquire after his fortune, if any. There was not quite enough room in the carriage for the sisters, however.

Thus it was that Miss Arabella found herself walking back to the cottage accompanied only by Miss Anna and Mrs. O'Keefe. They were but a few hundred yards down the road when it started to rain — an intense, drenching downpour that seemed to issue from a clear blue sky.

"It's another half a mile," Anna wailed, "and I haven't another dress!"

"But we are standing at the back pathway to Flanders House," said Arabella, and I see some kind of building but a stone's throw from here, nestled in the trees. "Surely, two bedraggled ladies and their servant may take refuge there without being considered improper."

"But you heard our uncle!" said Anna. "I'm not walking into such a den of iniquity!"

"Iniquity, or a ruined dress?" said Arabella. "I shall go alone."

"But what about Mrs. O'Keefe? She cannot divide herself in two, and neither of us can really be out and about without being properly chaperoned!"

"Decency be dashed," said Arabella — Mrs. O'Keefe squealed in shock — and started down the pathway towards Sodom and Gomorrah.

"Oh, bugger!" Anna exclaimed, and more, perhaps, but the pelting rain drowned out her voice.

4

Incense and Insensibility

The driving rain made it impossible to see where she was going, so Miss Arabella half-slid toward the first structure in her field of vision. It had an impressive door which she was barely able to pull open. When she set foot inside, she discovered that she was standing in an antechapel. Set upon an impressive plinth, a life-sized marble effigy of the Blessed Virgin Mary glared down at her. Behind her, there was an elaborate fresco depicting the temptation of Eve, and the first man and woman being driven from Paradise by an angel with a flaming sword. A gothic doorway led to the nave of a private chapel, from which there issued a billowing cloud of incense. The smell was so intense, Arabella almost choked. So this was the smell of popery!

A preternatural terror seized her. So many stories from her girlhood about popish plots to overthrow England — about obscene rites — dark superstitions! She knew there was nothing to fear, and yet — she thought, *I must flee this very instant* — but she could still hear the pounding of the rain. *I must not give in to these childhood fears,* she told herself. She stepped into the chapel proper.

The smell was overpowering yet not unpleasant, when one got used to it. To Arabella's surprise, it did seem to impose an aura of sanctity on the chapel. There were only a few pews. On the altar was a most decadent crucifix, tastelessly portraying Our Lord in abject agony. Behind was a gorgeous painting ... to Arabella's amazement, she recognized it as either a Rubens, or belonging to that school — representing the annunciation. Small stained glass windows cast a soft, rainbow light upon the pews and the stone floor, which was worn to hollows by centuries of Catholic footfalls.

Across from the altar there was an upper, railinged gallery, upon which stood a kind of wooden throne over which were suspended the arms of the Earldom. Doubtless that was where His Lordship would sit in solitary splendour during what passed for a church service amongst his people.

Arabella lost her fear, so fascinated was she by all the richness, the gilt, the ornate carving of the pews, the coat of arms of the Earl, showing an eagle regardant with a fleur-de-lys in its claws. "A Rubens! All this history," she murmured, "right next to Applethwaite, yet closed to me until today!"

"And you shall see more history, dear lady, now that I

have returned from Virginia."

She jumped. For a man had been kneeling in one of the pews. She had missed him completely, as the seat backs were so high.

When he stepped out into the aisle, she recognized him at once, for she had seen an engraving in the Chiswick *Observer* — along with an announcement that he intended to return to England. "Your Lordship!" she exclaimed, and curtsied, for surely title outranked religion.

"Do me the honour of addressing me as David," said the Right Honourable Tobias David Chrysostom George Mary Durham-St. Aubin-Borgnis, Ninth Earl of Little Chiswick and Viscount Blueborough.

"I couldn't possibly."

"Oh but it is what I am used to, for in the Americas, one's title is of little meaning, and it is rather by one's character and bearing that one wins respect." He added, "Though, as I am sure you have heard from all the scandalmongers, I have little character."

Bearing, however, he did possess in abundance. Indeed, he had an uncanny resemblance to Monsieur Clatoux, causing Arabella to speculate that their house guest might have used His Lordship's visage as a template for creating his terrestrial soma. The colours were different, for the Earl's hair was red, and his skin, of course, not blue, nor his ears pointed; but they could otherwise have been reckoned twins.

While Monsieur had been completed naked when Arabella first laid eyes on him, the Earl wore nothing but a dressing-gown, making Arabella's position even more untenable ... for to be found in a compromising situation with ... a *Catholic* ... was scarcely to be imagined.

"You, I take it," he continued, "must have at least something in common with me. For you have broken into my private chapel without an invitation — and curiosity has already overcome your diffidence. You are daring. I imagine you have a mind. You read. You recognized the Rubens ... doubtless from the Virgin Mary's ample and voluptuous depiction. Rubens loves female flesh, and cannot avoid the sensual even when portraying the spiritual."

"To be sure, I have never actually seen one," she said. "Only engravings."

"Why, I have three! No, two ... I remember now, I had to sell one to the King to pay a gambling debt. You shall see the other one now! It is in ... my private apartments."

"Should you have the temerity to invite me there unescorted, my Lord —"

"You would go willingly! Ah, how well I have judged you — a woman after my own heart."

"Your Lordship seems to know a great deal about me."

"Yet, I would know your name."

"I am Arabella Dorrit," she said, and before she knew it, His Lordship had stridden towards her and seized her hands in his own.

She trembled. "Do not presume," she said, "even though I am not your equal."

He laughed. "What do I care of such things? It's only the middle classes who are concerned with such trivialities. I shall have you at my ball, and I shall reserve the first place on your dance card. We have lost America to be sure, but you shall be my New Found Land."

"You are much skilled at turning a girl's head, Your Lordship."

"Aye, that I am. I have broken a dozen hearts ... I pray you, do not break mine."

At that moment, they heard a knocking at the door to the antechapel. His Lordship said, "Now I *must* leave you, for to be seen would mean you were compromised, however innocent this conversation may have been. Remain! I shall return presently, and in a more official capacity." The Earl then vanished through a side door to the left of the altar, which presumably led to the vestry.

When Anna arrived at the cottage, soaked to the bone, with Mrs. O'Keefe in tow, Mrs. Dorrit knew that she would have to act with despatch. "We must rescue Arabella before her own curiosity betrays her!" she said. She sent Japheth up to the big house to borrow their second-best barouche, and gathered up her troops to do battle.

"I will have to go," said Mr. Bumbry, "in case I need to invoke the Almighty to protect my niece."

"I should very much like to go," said Monsieur, "to see for myself what Mr. Bumbry has so picturesquely described as Sodom and Gomorrah."

"Well," Anna said, "I for one am simply too wet and miserable to go anywhere — and I've nothing to wear."

Mrs. Dorrit was glad her daughter at least knew her priorities; for there were enough people on hand to rescue her sister, but not enough money for a new dress.

The barouche *was* the second-best, and clanked miserably, but Japheth got the horses moving tolerably well, and the rainstorm had subsided; the countryside was once more bathed in luxuriant sunlight. Since the back pathway to Flanders House was right next to the Applethwaite estate, it was not exactly a long journey.

"I am amazed, dear brother," Mrs. Dorrit said, "that we have never had occasion to turn down that pathway."

"It is only my devotion to our family's reputation, and the avoidance of social disaster," Mr. Bumbry said, "that allows me to embark on this odyssey now."

Monsieur sat aft with the cook; it would not do to approach Flanders House without at least a minimal entourage. As they turned, they saw the first building, an elegant little Gothic chapel. Doubtless Arabella had taken refuge here. Leaving the barouche, Mr. Bumbry bore down on the chapel, his demeanour grim. He flung open the door and the entire party marched in.

Mrs. Dorrit looked at the frescoes and the statue of the Virgin and said, "Well, I don't see any carcasses of sacrificed babies."

"The incense," Monsieur said, "though heady, is not unpleasing."

Perhaps these people were not quite as bad as her brother would have his congregation believe, Mrs. Dorrit thought. Mr. Bumbry, however, stalked about, staring wildly, and seeming to choke at the scent of the incense. "Why, they probably have her chained in the cellar even as we speak, and are subjecting her to unspeakable abominations!"

"Chained, uncle?" said Arabella, emerging from the chapel proper. "I hardly think so."

"You've not been molested … compromised in any way?"

"Why, dear Uncle, I have been sheltering from the rain, entirely by myself," Arabella said sweetly. "Had anyone else appeared, I would undoubtedly have run back out into the rain and ruined my dress rather than risk any defilement of my good name."

To Mrs. Dorrit's dismay, her cook marched straight into the chapel and — horror of horrors — *genuflected!* Then she proceeded to *cross herself!* Mrs. Dorrit gasped at the idolatry. "I told you," said Mr. Bumbry. "Sodom, Gomorrah, and who knows what else."

"I find your prejudices most quaint," said Monsieur. "I have yet to see any substantial difference between your two schools of worship."

"Oh, how could you be expected to understand?" Mr. Bumbry raged. "It is these differences that are the very backbone of our Englishness!"

"And are Roman Catholics not English?" came a resonant voice from above. The party gazed up at the balcony to see the Earl himself, wearing his robes of office, resplendent on his seat of power. "Are we not as loyal to King and Country? And is the peerage not riddled with those of us who tiresomely would not follow the fashion of the times, and the dictates of such as Cranmer and Cromwell?"

Mr. Bumbry sputtered and was at a loss for words. "Your Lordship," Arabella said, "my uncle is not accustomed to being contradicted; pay him no mind, I pray."

"I understand that I was the subject of your sermon today, Mr. Bumbry — I presume. News travels fast in Catholic circles; we are, after all, an oppressed minority, persecuted in our own land."

"But you refuse to accept the truth as revealed in scripture, bowing down instead to some Italian potentate!" said Mr. Bumbry.

"The truth? Might I ask you, sir, *Quid est veritas?*"

Arabella chimed in, without needing to reflect, "John, 18:38." She continued, "*Ego nullam invenio in eo causam.*"

"I find no fault in him," translated the Earl. "Why, what a learned young woman. More learned than I, I fear, for I'm afraid I failed Latin at Eton ."

"Forgive my niece," Mr. Bumbry said. "My late brother had no sons, and so he allowed his daughter to aspire to the intellect of a man."

"I love a bluestocking," His Lordship said. "Especially a pretty one."

He rose from his seat and went to a spiral staircase in the back of the gallery. He descended into the nave, whereupon Mrs. Dorrit, in spite of herself, curtsied. An Earl was an Earl, after all. And, miracle of miracles, he *liked* her daughter. Would her immortal soul be a fair price to pay for riches and power in *this* life? But no. Mrs. Dorrit stopped herself from indulging such fond fantasies.

Mrs. O'Keefe was kneeling in the direction of the altar, muttering in Latin. She had managed to fish out a rosary from her capacious bosom. Monsieur Clatoux wandered about, admiring the art, and mumbled, "Rubens, Rubens," as he examined the altarpiece.

"I am Mrs. Dorrit," said Mrs. Dorrit. "My brother, Mr. Bumbry, you have already surmised. And this is Monsieur Clatoux, our visitor from overseas."

"*Sacré bleu!*" said the Earl.

"He doesn't like his complexion to be discussed," said Mrs. Dorrit in a stage whisper. "Hereditary illness, you know."

"He jests, mama," said Arabella. "Frenchmen only say that in bad novels."

"Indeed I do," said the Earl. "Which leads me to the point at hand. Who is going to introduce me to your lovely daughter … that I may set about paying court to her?"

5

Prawn and Pianoforte

... but we have not yet spoken of Miss Anna, except in passing. It was easy to dismiss Miss Anna as the more ungainly, awkward, and foul-mouthed of the twins. Yet, as Arabella never ceased to marvel, Anna had depths which she rarely chose to reveal.

Indeed, a few days after the incident at Flanders House, quite suddenly, she chose to open herself up to Monsieur Clatoux.

It occurred during another dull tea-time, with Arabella in the orchard, Mrs. Dorrit and Mr. Bumbry at tea, and Anna, once more, at the pianoforte, struggling through a nocturne by John Field. It was, as it happened, the very first one in the book, in E flat, requiring the smoothest possible movement of the left hand in groups of three, over which a simple but soaring melody was imposed.

Presently Miss Anna became aware that Monsieur was standing in the shadows, listening intently. "I don't like being spied on," she said.

Monsieur Clatoux said, "Why, my dear Miss Anna, do not stop playing on my account. I was rather enjoying your performance."

"How can you possibly say that?" Anna said. "I've heard it said that I have the rhythmic sense of a scullery maid frigging a pig."

"My! You do have a *penchant* for the colourful! Who could possibly have said such a thing to your face?"

Miss Anna laughed bitterly. "Not to my face. 'Twas our so-called footman, complaining to the maid-of-all-work, when he thought I wasn't listening."

"Yet you take such insults in good humour," said Monsieur. "That is admirable."

"My sister defends herself from an unfeeling world by flaunting her intelligence," Anna said. "I do so by concealing mine."

"Yet despite your lack of proficiency, it would appear that you love music."

"Very much, Monsieur Clatoux. Yet I can't seem to make my fingers do what I hear when I look at the printed page. I am sure Mr. Field would be squirming in his grave, were he to give ear to my efforts."

"In his grave! I hardly think so! He is alive, and still composing, in Russia."

"Russia? Whatever for?"

"Perhaps, as an Irishman, he could find a more appreciative reception in a country less coloured by prejudice against … what did your uncle call it … *popery*?"

Doggedly, Anna had another try at those opening arpeggios, her fingers getting all entangled.

"I can help," said Monsieur.

"Do not say that! No one can help me … no one has ever rescued me from anything … let alone myself!"

"Shush, dear Miss Anna. *He that hath ears to hear, let him hear.*"

"Ah … Matthew 11:15," Anna murmured. "I hadn't taken you for a religious man."

"I have been familiarizing myself with all the creations of your fascinating … as it were … civilization," Monsieur said. "I now understand that to be taken for a sober man of character, one must pepper one's conversation with quotations from this somewhat disjointed collection of curious and contradictory tales."

Miss Anna said, "Ah, but you must not say that quite so bluntly when you're in society, Monsieur Clatoux. Scripture is what binds us together."

"And also, it seems, what keeps you apart. Ah, but I so love your species! So primal! So innocent! Such blithe unawareness, such lack of introspection! It is beautiful! If any place in this galaxy could be called the Garden of Eden, I daresay it would be Little Chiswick."

He then proceeded to cover Miss Anna's ears in his massive blue hands. She uttered a little squeal, for the mere touch of Monsieur's firm, musky flesh upon her uncovered face filled her with a naughty delight. "Pray, do not cry out," Monsieur whispered urgently. "I do not mean to molest you … nay, rather to unlock a doorway to a deeper world. Close your eyes. Quick! I command it!"

"Strewth!" Miss Anna exclaimed. She attempted a horrified shudder, but was puzzled to find she was more thrilled than frightened. She closed her eyes, wondering if

Monsieur was planning an osculatory assault on her lips. Instead, something even more extraordinary happened.

She saw, in her mind's eye, the spiky little notes of John Field's nocturne. The notes danced in the air, they seemed to leap off the staff and to enter her eyeballs, to race through her veins like blood, and all at once her fingers became engorged with the prickly passion of cascading tones, and her hands pounced upon the pianoforte like a plummeting hawk, teasing at the keys and producing perfect triplets in the left hand while the right hand soared, as though Field were himself a field … a vast, verdant field over which she was being carried on currents of wind … ah, ah, what ecstasy!

"Monsieur Clatoux," she cried out, "what depredations are you inflicting upon my innocent person? Pleasure this acute cannot possibly be other than sin."

"I am merely opening your eyes and ears to perceptions that are already burgeoning out of the fertile soil of your febrile unconscious."

Abruptly, Monsieur released his hands from Anna's ears. Immediately, her sensations dulled. It was as if she had slipped from a cosmos of bright colours into a grey, drab plane of existence. "Oh!" she said. "I feel … depleted … empty." A terrible sadness possessed her, as overwhelming as the heights of ecstasy had been. "What has happened to me?"

"The link has broken."

Miss Anna tried a few chords on the pianoforte. As earlier today, as on every previous day that she had laboured to make music, the sounds that issued forth were tenuous and discordant.

Anna said, in confusion, "Are you telling me that I shall be able to play the pianoforte like a heavenly muse from henceforth … but *only* if you are standing behind me, covering my ears? Damn me if I shall perform in public in such a disgraceful fashion!"

"No. You will be able to reach that heightened state on your own. I shall teach you, Miss Anna. For though your sister has *learning*, you have *feeling*, though you hide it. You see … there is … a *force* that binds all entities in the universe, be they animate or inanimate … and you must tap into that force, you must feel it *flow* through your fingers."

All at once, Anna experienced an epiphany. "Why, it's *animal magnetism!* Yes, I have heard of that. My sister once read to me from the writings of Dr. Franz Mesmer. Monsieur, you are so very clever … so very modern … you are a *hypnotist!*"

"I suppose you could call it that."

Meanwhile, having finished her tea, Mrs. Dorrit was in the kitchen with the cook, for a most extraordinary thing was about to occur the next day. Word had come from the main house that Lord Chuzzlewit wished to visit his cousins, and an appropriate luncheon would have to be organized. Mrs. Dorrit wished to make sure that the repast was appropriate — elegant, and not overstated. It should not appear that the Dorrits were completely lacking in means, yet the cost of the ingredients could not really go beyond three shillings and sixpence.

On the floor, Pauline, the maid-of-all-work, was vigorously scrubbing some of the household's scant silver. Mrs.

O'Keefe had been able to obtain a parcel of prawns from the fishmonger; so fresh were they, indeed, that they were still jumping about in a tureen, ready to be boiled. The cook had been planning an inexpensive eel pie, to which the prawns might serve as a toothsome topping, with a light garnish of parsley — lending an exotic élan to the dish.

A curious dish, to be sure, but Mrs. Dorrit was planning to say that the dish was French. Who would know? And it would be in Monsieur's honour.

"Energetic little things, are they not?" said Mrs. Dorrit, deftly catching a prawn as it leapt, squirming, onto the counter.

"To be sure, ma'am," said the cook.

At that moment, the most extraordinary sound came from the drawing-room. It was music that was like a rushing river, a chill evening by candlelight, a wind in the tree-tops. "That cannot possibly be our Anna!" said Mrs. Dorrit.

"Aye, 'tis," said Mrs. O'Keefe, "for the Frenchman's been in to see her."

"But this playing is more than a maidenly accomplishment," said Mrs. Dorrit. "It's as if John Field himself were sitting at my instrument, squeezing ecstasy from every key … every … *pore!*" she continued, no longer sure which of her instruments she was alluding to. For she had but to close her eyes and a vision of Monsieur's fleshy, cerulean engine reared up in her mind's eye, flooding her senses with exquisite rapture tinged with some forbidden passion. She could feel a swoon coming on.

"Be careful, ma'am," said the cook, "or you'll collapse

into the prawns."

"Whatever can be wrong with me?"

"If I may be so bold, ma'am, there's naught that ails you, that could not be remedied with a sound tupping."

"Impertinence!" she said, yet smiled. "Is that all you Catholics ever think of?" She could not be angry, so ensorcelled was she by the searing music.

The music concluded with a resonant, rippling chord; and almost at once, Anna swept into the kitchen, her arms flailing triumphantly. "I've managed to … get in touch with my inner truth!" she said. "I've listened to the music of my heart!"

"Heavens," said her mother.

"Yes, mama! I shall play at Lord Chuzzlewit's next soirée! I shall overcome all resistance! I shall speak directly to their profoundest sensibilities! Mama, Monsieur has shown me a pathway toward ultimate truth!"

"What's got into her?" said Mrs. O'Keefe. "Why, she be skittish as a lamb!"

"Surely you rave, my dear," said Mrs. Dorrit, though she admitted to herself she had been much moved by the performance. "One nocturne is surely no epiphany. It could be an aberration." And yet … she had never seen her daughter thus. Even her ungainliness had lessened; she glowed.

"It is no aberration," said Monsieur, standing in the doorway of the kitchen. "Miss Anna shall surely impress His Lordship's friends and the most influential matrons of the ton, should she continue to play the pianoforte with such passion."

At that moment, Mrs. O'Keefe lifted the tureen of living

prawns and began to drop them, one by one, into a pot of boiling water.

Upon seeing this, Monsieur began to scream — no human scream, but a sound like the shrieking of a piccolo. His visage, already blue, darkened into a livid hue, and as he screamed a stream of bright blue vomit was expelled from his mouth. For a split second, his face transformed into that of a crustacean, with scales, spikes, and huge sapphire eyes with multiple facets. The metamorphosis was but momentary; the alien visage immediately transformed back into the same comely human features they were all familiar with.

Monsieur Clatoux's vomitus did not smell unpleasant. Rather, it had the same musky, sensuous fragrance that emanated from his entire form. Disgusting as it looked, Mrs. Dorrit also found it fascinating, for within it there wriggled minuscule blue organisms that bore a surprising resemblance to the prawns which had just suffered death by boiling. *Perhaps our Frenchman has some strange connection to these little morsels of the sea,* Mrs. Dorrit reflected.

It took Monsieur a few moments to calm himself. By then, the prawns were quite, quite dead, and a delicious shade of pink, as Mrs. O'Keefe strained the contents of the pot through a colander.

Pauline got up from polishing the silver and, mop in hand, made to attack the pile of writhing blue ejecta with a will. But this proved difficult, for the vomitus had a life of its own, skittering across the floor on a thousand tiny legs. As Pauline gasped, the entire writhing mass formed itself into a projectile and flew back into Monsieur Clatoux's open mouth. He swallowed with a loud, liquid gulp.

His entire body shimmered a little and in seconds had fully reverted to his elegant appearance. If anything, he seemed even more dashing than before, his billowing hair positively leonine, his fragrance more powerful, and his form fitting the late Mr. Dorrit's suit more perfectly than before.

"I do apologise for my most inappropriate behaviour," he said mildly. "I know they are not sentient, and quite unconnected to the galactic intelligence that pervades our species ... and yet ... as a result of a chance resemblance of your food animals to ... *my children* ..."

He paused. "Shall we continue to discuss tomorrow's luncheon?"

6

Love and Luncheon

Arabella had not witnessed the spectacle in the kitchen, and the description she had from her sister, mother, and the servants was confusing. Each thought they had seen a completely different event. "Poor Monsieur," the cook tsk-tsked, "he has an allergy, and may not even look at a prawn, let alone eat one." Her mama was going on and on about how Monsieur had changed shape — "He's a veritable Jupiter, becoming a swan, or a bull, or a lobster at will!" while Miss Anna rhapsodized about "The power! Oh, the all-encompassing splendour of the force!"

No one, in fact, thought to ask Monsieur Clatoux himself what had occurred. But Arabella undertook to do so as soon as there was a spare moment when she could question him uninterrupted.

It was during an early morning walk, in fact, when Monsieur revealed to Arabella just how unlike a Frenchman he was. "You have already guessed that I am not human," he said, as they perambulated among the apple trees, "but perhaps you haven't considered just *how* … alien … I am."

"I know you told Mama you had seven sexes," Arabella said, "but I'm afraid I am not entirely sure how that would … ah … work. In terms of … engineering, that is."

"The act of reproduction for us is, I have to admit, complicated. It can take years to complete every stage. Of course, we do not require all seven sexes at the same time. Rather, there are three pairs, of which one each must have amorous congress with the odd one out; and some of the sexes are actually different stages in the life cycle of the same individual, so one may occasionally change gender, depending on the exact chemical composition of the atmosphere at that moment, for our world experiences dramatic windstorms in which immiscible gaseous substances whirl around each other in a complex quadrille, changing the chemical composition of the planetary surface as they sweep over our dwelling places … and catalysing our metamorphoses from larva to nymph to hive-mind to somatic schism to chrysalis … and finally, yes, the end product is nonetheless still proposal, nuptials, property and the further propagation of the species, and so on, just as on Earth."

Arabella had to admit that, bluestocking though people might call her, even she had no idea what Monsieur was talking about, but she politely murmured vague noises of feigned understanding. "You seem to be describing the stages of a butterfly rather than a sentient being," she said, mystified.

"From an evolutionary point of view, I am somewhat

closer to a butterfly than to an ape," he said.

"What's an evolutionary point of view?"

"Ah, I've forgotten once more than I am stranded in time as well as space," he said. "I could simply give you the old 'godlike aliens with mysterious powers' routine, but you're far too intelligent for that. However, as I understand it, Lord Chuzzlewit is coming to luncheon. I shall reserve my scientific lecture for a more opportune moment."

"Oh! It would be so thrilling for you give such a talk to the Royal Academy!" she said.

"And as thrilling to see you seated amongst such luminaries as the Astronomer Royal," he said.

"Alas," Arabella said, shaking her head disconsolately,"t here is a limit to what is permitted to women," She continued, "And the right to listen in public to learned academic papers would make me a societal pariah. But I shall read it when it comes to the library, of course. His Lordship wishes to own every book ever published. He will demand yours."

Monsieur picked a low-hanging apple from the nearest tree and handed it to her.

"Was it not a woman who persuaded Adam to eat from the tree of knowledge?" he said, once again surprising her with how much he had managed to learn about the ways of the English in but a few days. "Do not demean your gender, though your society may do so. No sex is innately inferior. I should know, for I belong to a species that has seven of them. Sometimes more than seven — I shall explain the various possible permutations when we have a free moment."

It was just as well, thought Mrs. Dorrit, not to serve the prawns at all for luncheon. For what if Monsieur were to fetch up again? The visits of Lord Chuzzlewit were infrequent enough; nothing must go wrong. In fact, she made sure that Mr. Bumbry was not home — that he would make time to minister to some sick parishioners.

Nothing was going to ruin this luncheon! For if Anna's newfound skill at the pianoforte could be parlayed into an invitation to one of His Lordship's soirées … and so, just as a precaution, no prawns. And therefore, it was to be hoped, no cerulean vomitus.

After the sudden change of plans, Mrs. O'Keefe had managed to do up an eel pie, a brace of pigeon, and a venison stew. It was a homely repast, but the cook did have a way with condiments. Since the demise of Lady Chuzzlewit, the master of Applethwaite Manor had become something of a trencherman. He was no longer the dashing officer who told tales of having served with Nelson at the Battle of the Nile.

Mrs. Dorrit knew, of course, that the extent of her cousin's service with the admiral consisted of once, as a midshipman, having delivered to him a letter from his wife, for which service he had received a tuppenny tip. Somehow, this incident had evolved in the telling, and after a couple of decades, more details were still being added. She wondered what Monsieur would think if her cousin started with his war tales, which were mostly reconstructed from stories he had heard in his year at Portsmouth, running petty errands for his superior officers — little different, no doubt, from young Japheth for his mother the dowager — and wearing an equally silly costume.

Luncheon passed with little incident. Mrs. Dorrit was dreading the conversation, because at some point, if he did not launch into a war story, she knew, Lord Chuzzlewit was bound to make some cutting remark to put her in her place, since she was entirely dependent on his charity for a place to live and an allowance to live on. But Monsieur provided such sterling diversion that His Lordship missed several opportunities for gratuitous condescension.

"Ah," Monsieur would say, "the joys of travel! The stars streaming past one, bourne through the vastness of space on the wings of the cosmos ... the wonders of the universe ... the exotic animals and vegetation ... the strange races ... the anthropophagi ... and men whose heads do grow beneath their shoulders ..."

"You have such a way with words," said Lord Chuzzlewit. "Your description of your travels puts me in mind of my own voyage to Egypt, some years ago. We have much in common."

"Though those last two things you said *were* pilfered straight out of Shakespeare's *Othello*," said Anna.

Why could that girl not think before she spoke? Mrs. Dorrit thought. She had more to gain out of this luncheon than anyone else, yet could she not refrain from blurting out the truth at inopportune moments?

"I have heard," said Monsieur mildly, "that in your country, to quote from the Bard of Avon is esteemed almost as highly as a reference to the Bible." He had smoothed over Anna's solecism completely.

"Such a wit! Why, my dear Emma, the man's a charmer!" Lord Chuzzlewit said. "Your intellect, sir, is most sharp for a Frenchman! But, while not meaning to be rude, we also do hear rumours of an immense fortune, Monsieur Clatoux. Pray tell us whether you plan to remain in Little Chiswick for the season. Perhaps we have among us a candidate or two to be considered for the role of ... ah ... *Madame* Clatoux."

"Monsieur has told me that his interest in our marriage customs are purely academic," said Mrs. Dorrit.

"Indeed, my Lord," said Monsieur, "for it is indeed the case that we have no marriage as you know it in my country at all."

"Ha, ha! No marriage in your country! You all live in sin, then!"

"In a manner of speaking."

"Why, the man's a fountain of wit! I can imagine him entertaining crowned heads in a cap and bells!"

Now, sensing that it was time for a change of pace, Mrs. Dorrit decided it was time to announce the *pièce de résistance*. "Let us retire to our humble parlour," she said, "for my daughter Anna will play the pianoforte for us ... whilst we sip some ... *coffee*," uttering the name of that costly elixir with the breathless enthusiasm she felt it must deserve.

"Heavens," said Lord Chuzzlewit. "Coffee!"

"Monsieur has procured a small supply of the beans," Mrs. Dorrit said, "from a most unusual source."

"Ah! You have been to Turkey?" said Lord Chuzzlewit. "Your guest, my dear Emma, is a treasure indeed!"

Mrs. Dorrit did not mention that the beans had been squeezed, like the golden guineas, from Monsieur's own "adjustable protoplasm." Rather, Mrs. Dorrit whispered in her cousin's ear, "I have been told it has remarkable qualities in its ability to revitalize the, ah, masculine potency of a man."

"Strewth! Enough chatter! When will I be permitted to perform upon the bloody pianoforte?" Anna said, impatiently rising from the table.

Presently, His Lordship was ushered, by Japheth, to the late Mr. Dorrit's favourite *fauteuil*. Although the drawing-room was shabby compared to anything in the manor proper, Mrs. Dorrit had always endeavoured, with the help of just her three servants, to keep the room neat and dusted. Arabella served coffee to Lord Chuzzlewit herself, hoping her sister's outburst would soon be forgotten. For, she reflected, high and mighty though His Lordship might be, they were still *en famille,* and a certain informality might be forgiven at times.

"My sister is anxious," she said. "She has been practising for weeks."

"I've heard she plays atrociously," said His Lordship. "And her manners are, to say the least, common. But we are family, of sorts. Though your great-great-grandmother *did* behave somewhat indelicately and, one might remark, on the left side of the coverlet."

"Your Lordship!" Arabella exclaimed. For this century-old blot on the escutcheon of the Dorrit branch of the family was never spoken of, especially in mixed company. But Lord Chuzzlewit merely laughed, so heartily that his jowls quaked.

Miss Arabella feared for her sister, for so much was at stake in this performance. And when the air was rent by a thunderous dissonance, and she saw that Anna was pounding the keys with the grace of a blacksmith shaping a horseshoe, she began to panic. For this was indisputably the most horrifying travesty of John Field that it was possible to imagine. The melody did not soar; nay rather it plummeted to the carpet on wings of lead. There was at least one false note in every harmony, and the rhythms, far from the smooth triplets written in the printed music, sounded like the canter of a three-legged pony.

Indeed, there was a loud crash from the kitchen, for Mrs, O'Keefe had let some priceless porcelain heirloom drop to the floor, and the clatter was followed by a piercing cry of "Blessed Mother Mary and all the Saints above!"

Arabella half expected His Lordship to excoriate them all for the sounds of popish hocus-pocus in the very home of the Reverend Lionel Bumbry, but he did not. Indeed, he appeared to be completely ensorcelled by Miss Anna's rendition.

The explanation was clear. For standing behind His Lordship's armchair stood Monsieur Clatoux. His hand was stretched out over Lord Chuzzlewit's pate, and a soft blue light played like a halo around his face. From his thumb and little finger, jagged bolts of blue light gushed forth, one into each of Lord Chuzzlewit's ears. It was clear that their cousin was hearing a wholly different performance from the one that jangled so unnervingly about the drawing-room.

Miss Arabella sat amazed at His Lordship's demeanour. For his eyes stared straight up, practically rolling into their sockets, as though he saw past the petty harshness of their world into the benevolent visage of the Almighty Himself.

As Miss Arabella watched, it seemed that the auditory hallucination — if such it was — seemed to rippled outward, from the face of Lord Chuzzlewit. When it reached her own ears, she cried out, startled, felt warm tears spring unbidden. She looked at her mother; at first, her expression was frozen in a soundless scream, yet when the magical wave of sound reached her, her gaping horror turned to wonder. Mrs. O'Keefe's horrified utterances were transformed, blending into the symphony like an angelic melisma.

The music swept over them like a tempest; when it subsided, there was a soft clanging, a note of pain that shot through the memory like lost love.

"Surely," Lord Chuzzlewit murmured, "we have heard the Seraphim and the Cherubim before the very throne of God."

Monsieur snatched away his hand. It seemed that they all awoke from some kind of trance. Anna went on playing, with indifferent skill, for a few more moments, then, realizing that the magic was over, stopped in mid phrase. "I'm terribly sorry," she said. "I'm simply dreadful, aren't I?"

"On the contrary, my dear," said Lord Chuzzlewit. "I was transported."

"To Australia?" Anna said, dourly. "I was that bad?"

"No, no, my dear, dear girl ... I was not transported as a convict to Australia... but as a slave to perfect beauty ... to Heaven!"

"Goodness!" said Anna, for once not swearing.

"And I'm not just saying that because you're my third cousin once removed."

And this was the most remarkable thing about this luncheon — not the miraculous performance by Arabella's sister, nor the transmutation of alien flesh into Turkish coffee beans — but the fact that His Lordship had deigned to acknowledge his kinship with the most impoverished, shopworn and least significant branch of his illustrious family.

7
Soirée and Survival

It need only be said that Anna's rendition of the nocturnes of John Field at Lord Chuzzlewit's soirée was a triumph, and much spoken of in the days to come.

It was Arabella alone who noticed how much effort Monsieur Clatoux had expended in making Anna's recital a success. She herself had given a performance, an impressive recitation of Hecuba's lament from the play of the same name by Euripides, in the original Greek.

As she had undertaken to learn the Erasmian pronunciation of ancient Greek — which differed substantially from the pronunciation taught to young gentlemen in school (if Greek, in these ill-educated modern times, was deemed worthy to be taught at all) — she managed the singular achievement of not being understood by a single person in the room.   Nonetheless, she undertook, by means of swooping and swooning, of passionate apostrophe and bouts of howling, whining, and weeping, to elicit a satisfactory volume of applause from the audience, once they realized that her performance was over.

It was not actually difficult to know that her ten minutes of Greek had ended, for so moving were Euripides's words, and so profoundly did she empathise with the suffering of Troy's dispossessed queen, that she did not feign her fainting spell at the end, but fell to the carpet with a thump, hearing but the beginning of the prolonged clapping and bravos that followed.

She came to her senses in the library of the manse.   To her infinite joy, she was alone in her favourite room in the entire estate.   They must have brought her there when she passed out.   There was no fear about her being compromised by being alone; she was, after all, a relation of the master of the house, if only a poor relation, and she was not important enough for anyone here to be concerned with her being compromised.

Her mind a blur, she managed to drag herself up from the leather divan she had been placed on.   The room was dark, the only light source a lamp glowing on the carved oak desk.   Around her, thousands of tomes, beautifully bound in matching green leather; and a few shelves of recent acquisitions, some with the pages still uncut, for Lord Chuzzlewit was a collector, not a reader.

Picking up the lamp, she walked over to the shelf of the latest arrivals.   She was wondering whether there were any new scientific journals. Perhaps the Astronomer Royal had observed in the night sky one of the selfsame star-faring vessels that Monsieur Clatoux had arrived in. But she found only silly women's novels. Unopened, unbound, the pages still attached to each other, with paper bindings, these books had not yet been sent to the bindery. *A veritable cornucopia of women's rubbishy fantasies*, she thought. *Look at them all!* Sense and Sensibility? Pride and Prejudice? *What ludicrous titles.* She wondered who the author, credited merely as "a Lady," was. Doubtless, some frustrated, wishful-thinking member of the lower middle classes.

At length, she found a slim volume that seemed far more interesting. *An account of certain anomalous observations in the night sky over Greenwich,* she read, *written by an interested member of the Academy, who shall remain anonymous.*

How exciting! She picked up the book and was disappointed to see that the pages had not yet been cut. No worries. She had seen a paperknife on the desk. She did not think anyone would notice that this little pamphlet had been cut open. She went over to the desk with her prize, and, her hands trembling with the anticipation of it, sat down to slice open the first signature. The text was not even in Latin, so probably was not written by a real scientist.

This author holds the possibility to be at the very least plausible, and well within the bourne of human conjecture, that amongst the multitudinous creations of the Almighty there might be in existence worlds beyond the sublunary constraints of the terrestrial, and that upon such worlds might dwell creatures, perhaps yet unfallen from divine grace and free of original sin....

Miss Arabella was just turning the page when the strains of a John Field nocturne filled the air.

Nay, at the first, the sound was as noisome as the caterwauling of a dozen felines. It was, Arabella realized, the audience, reacting in horror to the bloody massacre of Lord Chuzzlewit's four-hundred-guinea Italian pianoforte. But abruptly, from the jangling discords and chaotic shrieking, there emerged wholly different sound.

It was a music of such understated stillness that the audience was instantly silenced. It was even more beautiful than when Anna had played for His Lordship in the vicar's drawing-room. The nocturne crescendoed, from the barest whisper to a thunderous roar. It was impossible to believe that a mere pianoforte could sound like ... an entire orchestra and choir. Arabella looked up from the — admittedly dry — scientific paper. Cascading chords washed over her in waves.

Arabella went to the door. When she opened it, the flood of sound was overwhelming. She found herself walking toward the source of it, her feet almost seeming to float above the carpet. She crossed a hallway, passed a sweeping double staircase, all the while drawn by the music. Presently she found herself at the open portal of the drawing-room.

The seats were all filled, so she did not enter the room. Indeed, she durst not, for the guests were all so enthralled, so ensorcelled, that to elbow her way inside might have been deemed sacrilege. And so it was that, standing in the doorway, she was the only one to see what Monsieur Cla-toux was doing.

He was right inside the doorway, so none of the guests could see him. His arms were upraised. His hands were spread out, and blue jagged light was dancing from his fingertips. He waved his arms, and it was as though all the guests were being controlled by a master puppeteer.

Arabella did not think that Monsieur was capable of sweating, but he was under tremendous strain. Were he human, he would have been drenched in perspiration … she was quite sure of it. But the nocturne was only half done. It had several minutes to go.

"Monsieur!" she whispered. But he was too deep in concentration to respond. Arabella sensed the power he was tapping into, almost as if she were connected to him by some supernatural force. She felt the power exploding from within him, bursting out through his fingers, reaching into the souls of the audience. For a second, she seemed to touch their very thoughts.

Mrs. Faversham, who was fussing about whether the rabbit stew she had left to simmer overnight would be burnt when she arrived home. Mr. Stafford-Jones, remembering how he once peered inside his niece's unmentionables. Lady Bradbury, savoring her first cup of imported chocolate. Little Gregory Chuzzlewit, desperately trying to memorize the second aorist of *apothnésko*. All these humdrum thoughts, like brightly coloured fish, snared in the net of Anna's playing.

Suddenly, Monsieur let out a huge sigh and slumped back. He fell straight into Arabella's arms, and, immediately aware of the unconscionable breach of propriety, she stepped back, further into the hall, with Monsieur writhing in her unproffered embrace. To her astonishment, the audience did not turn around. Anna's performance continued to exert its magic.

"She's finally able to use the force herself," said Monsieur, still squirming and making whiny animal noises, like a frightened mouse. "I was able to let go. Not a moment too soon! Miss Arabella, I pray, get me outside into the open air, instanter! Else I shall perish!"

Finding a reserve of strength that surprised her, Arabella dragged the Frenchman out, through the hall, past the sweeping staircase, to a back door.

She held on to Monsieur as he staggered and shambled around in the garden. Presently, coming to an ornate swing whose seat was cunningly wrought with images of roses and angels, which glinted in the moonlight, she was able to ease Monsieur into position.

He gasped. "Thank you, Miss Arabella," he said. "I'm well aware of the risks you took in bringing me out here, unchaperoned."

"Sir, I did not even consider that, so concerned was I about your condition. And my sister's performance — perhaps it has fallen apart by now?"

"It has not," he said. "I have been but a catalyst for her to unleash the mental powers she already possesses. I was but the flame on the fuse; Miss Anna was the cannon."

"But you have expended so much energy ...."

"It is true. I pray you, push the swing a little. I need ... a great deal of air."

Arabella did so, noting that the sheer act of breathing seemed to bring Monsieur Clatoux's spirits back a little.

"Your atmosphere … it contains trace amounts of the inert gases that I need to fuel my programmable protoplasm … I have a desperate need of argon … krypton … xenon … only one part in ten million in the air of your world … swinging allows me to absorb it faster…"

"I confess, Monsieur, I haven't the slightest notion what you mean. Those fanciful words … krypton … xenon … they all sound like wondrous substances from ancient Greek myth — like moly and ambrosia! But if swinging restores you to health, why, I shall push the swing as hard as I can."

She pushed the swing and Monsieur Clatoux's visage, in the moonlight, glowed a more brilliant blue than she had seen it in days.

"I forget," said Monsieur Clatoux, "that these gases will not be discovered for some decades on your world. I should not have mentioned them, lest I unleash a … ah, the infinite paradoxes of time! The glorious chaos of the relativistic multiverse!"

His rhapsody left her as befogged as before.

"Swing harder, my dear!" As she did, a curious glowing machine seemed to crawl out of Monsieur's nostrils. It was shaped like a funnel, and it was sucking in huge volumes of air as the Frenchman swung back and forth. Suddenly, they seemed to be at the centre of a whirlwind and the the air was brisk, nay, chilly.

"What is happening?" said Miss Arabella.

"Oh! 'tis but a fractional distillation device, designed to extract the inert gases out of the atmosphere. It will not harm you."

At length, Monsieur signalled that Miss Arabella could stop. She was sweating profusely and her garments were a little out of kilter from her exertions. She was well aware that this did not look good, and that soon, the other guests would perhaps be emerging from the soirée to take the air in the gardens. She could already hear some distant chatter. And while she herself was not concerned with being seen alone with a man, she was cognisant of how her mother would feel to have all hope of a proper match thwarted by gossip.

Yet, she sensed that Monsieur was in direr straits than he would admit.

"Come," she said, "we will walk back and blend in with those emerging from the mansion. But you must tell me … how disastrous your condition really is."

"Miss Arabella," said Monsieur, "I am far from home, and subsisting on strange nutrients. My need for these gases will only increase."

"Ah! So you need a place where you can be hurled swiftly through the air! Why, at the London Mechanical Museum, but a brief barouche ride from Little Chiswick, there is a mechanical carousel. It's very modern. It has a mechanical organ which, when it plays a tune, causes horses to move about in a circle. The faster the tune, the quicker the rotation. It was built by a Belgian inventor of automata, a Monsieur Merlin. If we could manage to set you upon one of the horses, and set it to spinning to a merry quadrille —"

"My dear Miss Arabella! Even on this forsaken world, your species strives to be playful at the very limits of its primitive technology! Yet such a contrivance might extend my life for days, weeks, even. Perhaps even to the end of the season!"

"Your life?" Arabella said, alarmed.

"I'm afraid so," said Monsieur Clatoux. "For unless I repair my ship, I shall surely die."

8

Tea and Telephony

It was now time to prepare for the opening event of the season in earnest. For the Earl of Little Chiswick, Catholic though he might be, was still, by far, the most powerful personage in those parts, and his invitation could not be ignored. A season opening meant, of course, new clothes; indeed, Mrs. Dorrit had not allowed her daughters to attend the previous season's events at all, lest someone remember their dresses from the year before.

This year would be different, she was sure. Was not Monsieur Clatoux a limitless source of golden guineas? To this end, she once again borrowed the second-best barouche from the big house and trundled up her daughters, along with Monsieur himself, to the village of Little Chiswick.

There was not much to this hamlet — an inn, a modest village hall, and a few shops. There were rival dressmakers, on either side of a tea-shop.

As the barouche drew close, Mrs. Dorrit said, "I think it is best if I take Arabella to Madame Beaumarchais's shop, and Anna to the establishment of Signora Pirandello. This way, the two girls can enjoy an undivided experience, and not feel that they be rivals in trying to outdo the other."

"I certainly understand," said Monsieur Clatoux. "I myself have seven thousand siblings, so such family politics are most familiar to me."

Mrs Dorrit was carefully stepping over a steaming pyramid of equine manure that lay in her path. As always, when Monsieur said something outrageously impossible, she assumed it was just the language barrier.

"I can't help noticing," said Monsieur, "how your girls are so adept at not stepping into dung."

She said with pride, "They've learned that skill through trial and error throughout their childhoods, for I made them clean their own shoes and stockings if they were ever besmirched."

"And because of that, they cross the cobblestones with the the grace of dancers."

"Oh, you Frenchmen, so *méchant*! Always the *ballet*."For Frenchmen's thoughts were ever obsessed with lewdness. Mrs. Dorrit had heard of how French women danced half naked in the orgies of the Versailles. No wonder they'd had a revolution! "And now, Monsieur, since you have come to be a member of our family, might you chaperone Arabella for a moment, while I take Anna to the dressmaker's? Perhaps you shall take tea next door, at the Silver

Swan. It is, I think, a sufficiently public venue as to allow no hint of scandal, and I know that you are practically an uncle to the girls now."

Mrs. Dorrit showed Monsieur, with Arabella walking behind, to the entrance of the tea-shop, and made sure they were comfortably seated by the window, so that no impropriety could be implied. She then entered Signora Pirandello's. The signora had once been a great beauty, and a singer, who had as a very young woman performed in the operas of Mr. Handel, before being injured in a behind-the-scenes knife fight between rival divas; a half-century later, an elfin little woman with a stentorian voice, with Italian opera long since out of fashion, she had parlayed her knowledge of stage costuming into a little atelier with her late husband. She wore a black dress, having been in mourning for nigh on thirty years.

"Ah," said the dressmaker, looking up from her bolts of cloth. "We don't see you very often, Mrs … ah … Dorrit, is it not? I am so forgetful in my old age."

"Why, your memory is perfect," Mrs. Dorrit said, concealing her annoyance that the Italian had remarked on her long absence, which was doubtless a snide reference to her reduced circumstances.

"I don't need a dress," Anna said. "It's an inordinate waste, and I shall probably wear it but once."

"A lovely woman *needs* a dress," said Signora Pirandello.

"All the more reason I do not," said Anna, "for 'tis plain that *I* am plain; I am quite, quite plain."

"That, as every devoted mother knows, is in the eye of the beholder." She looked at Mrs. Dorrit. "But you would assuredly not pay a visit to this establishment, one that belongs to an Italian of the papist persuasion, who was indeed once married to a Semite — albeit a converted one — unless you had come into a little something."

"Oh, Mother," Anna said. "She sees right through you! I've always told you that tradesmen are much more perceptive than their class would seem to indicate."

As always, Mrs. Dorrit reflected, a day with Anna was going to be a trying day. She looked forward to taking Arabella to Madame Beaumarchais.

Miss Arabella's tea-time conversation with Monsieur was, indeed, a great deal more congenial. For one thing, there was no need to keep up the pretence of Monsieur Clatoux being a Frenchman.

Monsieur was not an avid tea drinker — this was perhaps the most alien-seeming thing about him, even more than the blue skin and pointed ears. Rather than adding milk and sugar, he imbibed it unadulterated, sipping it from a tea-spoon as though it were a miniature cup of soup. Arabella knew that people were watching, but they simply attributed such antics to his being a foreigner, not a creature from another world. And it was this other world that Arabella yearned to know about. And then there was the matter of Monsieur's ill health.

"The contraption in the London Mechanical Museum," she said. "We must contrive to visit it. I shall tell my mother and we will make a family outing of it. No one need suspect that for you it is a matter of such grave import."

"I fear that even a larger supply of the noble gases may not keep me going much longer. And your mother's thirst for gold is surpassed only by my body's need for trace elements."

"She thinks your powers are unlimited, I'm afraid. Alas, my mother has no more understanding of science than any other woman."

"Present company excepted, I assume."

Arabella laughed at this.

"Though we may find the substances needed to extend my life for a few days ... even weeks ... I must communicate with those of my kind. Only they can make it possible to repair my starship. I know that now."

"But how would that even be possible? I can send a letter as far as Whitehall for threepence ... but to the very stars?"

"We have devices," Monsieur said, "that enable us to communicate across the immeasurable vastness of space ... and, in a sense, even time itself. For the light from your sun takes eight minutes to reach us, and four years to travel even to the closest star. But our messages can fold that distance to an instant, as easily as one might fold a love letter before sealing it."

"Speaking at a distance? Even between the stars? I cannot imagine it."

"Ah, Miss Arabella, there are so many wonders as yet unseen in your world. Had I but all the time in the universe, what I would not tell you!"

"How can you? What you have just described ... why, there is not even a word for the art of casting one's voice over such distances … for how far is the sun? At least a thousand miles, I would think!"

"Ninety-three million, to be precise."

That was a number beyond imagining. Arabella trembled even to hear it. "If there was a word for it, a *scientific* word, it would have to come from Greek. The art of casting one's voice far, far away … *telephony.*"

"What a euphonious appellation!" said Monsieur. "Telephony, eh!"

Arabella continued, "My mother has two years' gossip to catch up with! She will never emerge from the Signora's. By the time she is ready to take me to Madame Beaumarchais, the afternoon will have slipped away quite! What shall we do? We cannot sip tea for another two hours."

"Perhaps we can perambulate about the village?"

"Why not? It is a public space."

Presently, then, Arabella found herself promenading with Monsieur Clatoux, unchaperoned, in the general environs of the tea-shop. She did not really mind about being seen. Her intellect was a bigger scandal than any compromise could be.

Miss Arabella showed her guest the village's meagre sights: a fragment of a Roman wall, overgrown with vines; a statue of an equestrian knight; a fountain. They stopped in front of the village hall.

"It is not used very much," said Arabella, "but it does house the few rare treasures we have here. Aside from the piece of Roman wall we have already visited, there are also some painted amphorae that were recovered from a villa. And an ancient stone that was once venerated by Celts …

it fell from Heaven a thousand years ago, according to the local legend."

"A meteorite?" said Monsieur.

"One would presume so," Miss Arabella said.

"I must examine it," he said. "I simply *must*."

"Then we shall," she said, for the front door of the village hall was unlocked, like every public building in Little Chiswick. She opened it and they entered. The hall had once been some kind of barn, for, a couple of centuries ago, the Earl's estates had been even bigger than they were now. Land had been lost by a succession of incompetent heirs, not to mention that some scions of the Earldom had fled to countries more friendly to Catholics, allowing unscrupulous managers control over the Comital Treasury. A gothic façade was now the entrance.

Within, it was dark and gloomy. Not a person in sight. Except for the centre of the hall, where the legendary rock was displayed on a plinth, illumined by a dustmote-filled shaft from a skylight. The rock sparkled; for while it was mostly black, there were iridescent flecks embedded in it.

Monsieur became tremendously agitated at the sight of the rock. More than agitated. His face actually started to glow, and his fingers were shaking ... nay, quivering, as though they were made of aspic.

"Rare earths," he murmured, as though the words were sweet nothings in a lover's ear.

"Rare earths?"

"Miss Arabella ... you must help me. I *must* possess that stone! That stone contains rare earths ... metals forged in the violent heart of an exploding star! It is those metals that I need to be able to calibrate the subetheric causality streams to enable this ... *telephony* to occur!"

"*Mon cher monsieur!* Are you asking me to ... become a thief ... a criminal?"

"Well ... my brief experience in your society has revealed an important truth ... that the authorities only punish felonies when they are committed by the lower classes."

"True enough. We haven't had a revolution, unlike the benighted French; there's no fear of *égalité* rearing its ugly head in Little Chiswick." She picked up the rock, which was considerably heavier than she had anticipated. "Catch!" she said, lugging it at him.

"So you will help me?" He caught the meteorite easily by thinning out his hand until it resembled a butterfly net.

"That is a clever trick," Arabella said, "but you can't very well leave the hall with your hand stretched out like that! And your clothes have nowhere in which to conceal such a huge rock," she went on. "On the other hand, I can easily hide it in my unmentionables, clamping it between my thighs. Fortunately, my capacious skirts are actually designed for concealment." She tucked the rock in. Walking was a little awkward, but she managed.

"My word," said Monsieur Clatoux. "I do believe I am feeling a glimmer of hope."

"I ... the mousy little bluestocking ... a common thief! Why, the thrill of it — the very thrill! My blood is racing!"

"I shall build my device!" said Monsieur excitedly. "I shall be healed in your Mechanical Museum, and in no time, I shall *telephone* home!"

9

Unmentionables

If Mrs. Dorrit expected that Arabella's visit to Madame Beaumarchais would be as time-consuming as Anna's had been at Signora Pirandello's, she was mistaken. Arabella met her at the door of the Frenchwoman's shop, and there was something most peculiar about her gait; she was ... waddling. *Perhaps no one else would have noticed it, but,* she reflected, *I* am *her mother.*

For a moment, a wild thought entered her mind ... perhaps Monsieur had somehow managed to ... she closed her eyes. Immediately, her memory conjured up an image of their first meeting, when Monsieur Clatoux had appeared entirely ... without a stitch of clothing. And she had caught a glimpse of ... that monstrosity of a blue appendage. Could it really be that the application of this engorged device to a woman's nether regions could render her incapable of proper deportment? She shuddered ... yet a part of her could not help but feel a kind of vicarious thrill.

No! She cleansed the thought from her mind. How repugnant, that she could even have thought it! And what opportunity could there have been for anything untoward to have occurred? They were never even alone together; they had had tea, then promenaded in the street, before every set of prying eyes in the village.

In any case, she knew that Arabella was a good girl. Why, rather than suffer a fate worse than death, she would probably have stabbed herself with the nearest sharp object. As she was visibly not dead, she had probably not been compromised in any fashion.

Putting aside her misgivings, Mrs. Dorrit left Anna with Monsieur in the tea-shop and prepared for another barrage of gossip from the usually garrulous Madame Beaumarchais. But the minute they entered the shop, Arabella held out her hand as though to ward off the devil, and said, "Mama, dearest, I shall entirely trust your taste in this matter. You know I care not a fig about my attire, and I am sure you know best when it comes to linens, muslins, and silks. Select anything you like."

"*Quelle horreur!*" Madame Beaumarchais ejaculated.

"No, no, my mind's made up. I shall wear whatever costume Madame cares to conjure up."

"Is there a price limit?" said the dressmaker, looking extremely pleased with herself.

"My dearest daughter," said Mrs. Dorrit, "this is your first opportunity to be properly seen, inspected, admired, sought after by the bachelors of the ton.   Poor girl, in another year you'll be deemed an old maid."

"Mama," said Miss Arabella, "I'm not even nineteen!"

"Precisely why we must hasten to see you settled, my dear."

"Indeed," Arabella said with some bitterness, "for what use are my intellectual skills, my linguistic prowess, and my encyclopaedic knowledge of literature and history — if I can't use these accomplishments to entrap some wealthy simpleton?"

"Very well, my dear. I shall choose for you," said Mrs. Dorrit, since her daughter was clearly not to be moved.

The sun was quite low when they returned to the cottage, to find Mr. Bumbry deep in the throes of composition, for it would be Sunday soon, and the ball at Flanders House was less than a week away. A fiery sermon was doubtless in preparation, and Mr. Bumbry was pacing up and down in the orchard, reading it aloud to an obsequious Japheth.   Arabella could make out such potent words as "abomination," "concupiscence," and "brimstone" interspersed amid the raving.

Mr. Bumbry stopped to glance at his nieces.

"Babylon's temptations have proved too much, I see," he said. "Ordering gowns for the ball, doubtless! Soon you shall be braving the iniquitous Hell that is Flanders House!"

"My dear brother," said Mrs. Dorrit. "You know very well that the requirements of the next world must needs give way before the needs of the present one. And every bachelor in four counties will be present at the Earl's ball!

And … unlike in other years, we have actually been *invited* … meaning that we have a chance to increase our standing in the ton … and that goes, dear brother, for *your* standing as well!"

"Oh, stop arguing, you two!" Anna protested. Arabella noted that her sister, even more than she, found the endless bickering of her mother and uncle too much to bear. "Surely you would not have two splendid bespoke gowns go to waste!   Thanks to Monsieur's magnanimity, we've been able to spend seven guineas on clothing —"

"Oh, the vulgarity!" said Mrs. Dorrit. "We must *never* discuss *money!*"

"Bugger vulgarity!" said Miss Anna, who seemed secretly quite pleased at how shocked the others were, though surely they were used to her linguistic extremes. "I'm going to go back to my pianoforte."

"I shall see whether Mrs. O'Keefe has anything for Mr. Bumbry," said her mother. "He must be famished after all that fire-breathing."

"Well, then, Mama, I shall take the air for a moment," said Miss Arabella,"before I go in to dinner."

"By yourself?" said her mother.

"Monsieur Clatoux shall defend me from any lewd gentlemen lurking in the bushes." For, to be sure, clamping a meteorite between her thighs had not been an easy task, especially when crowded into a barouche. Indeed, she worried that it might have become lodged somewhere in her unmentionables.

"Oh, very well," said Mrs. Dorrit. "We are, I suppose, *en famille.*"

Thus it was that Miss Arabella found herself alone with Mr. Clatoux.

"Quick," he whispered urgently. "Before we are discovered, we must pry loose that piece of space debris from your intimate parts."

Miss Anna played the pianoforte for a while, but she was distracted, and the dissonances came back, making her head ache terribly. At length, she heard Mrs. O'Keefe call out from the kitchen. It was time for supper. It was not a meal that was served every night at the vicarage, but as the family had missed the opportunity to have dinner together, with all the time spent in the village and Mr. Bumbry fulminating in the orchard, the cook had thrown together a modest repast of eel pie and leek soup.

"Go fetch your sister," said Anna's mother. "She'll catch a chill."

Anna went into the garden and saw no one. She called Arabella's name. When there was no response, Anna threaded the bushes and went through to the orchard. She did not see her sister.

But in the clearing, in the bright starlight, Monsieur Clatoux's vessel stood. It sparkled … it seemed almost alive. It was a thing of luminescent beauty, casting a pale blue glow over the clearing. And then there was the doorway … fleshy, puckering, not unlike a … decency forbade her from contemplating it.

But the doorway was different now. It was partially dilated.

Anna crept up to the opening and peered inside.

The door expanded even more. She was able to step inside. The walls of the ship were metallic, but also somehow alive. They rippled with a blue-green sheen, and tentacles and pseudopods formed and unformed, reaching out to claw at the air then being sucked back into the wall again. The room glowed with a sourceless light. It was wider than one might have imagined from looking at the outside.

"Strewth!" she said softly.

She tried calling Arabella's name, but her voice was drowned out by a thrum from the ship itself, the sound peppered with squeaks and squeals like an ungreased machine.

Miss Anna stepped further into the room. Suddenly, wrenching her stomach, she found herself walking up the wall like a spider. In a flash, sideways became down, and the floor had mutated into the wall.

And there was a corner that had not been there before. Anna heard a woman whimpering. She was almost certain it was Arabella's voice.

Then came the smooth tones of Monsieur. She could not tell where the voices came from, for direction seemed to have no meaning here.

"Relax, relax," he was saying, "I am sure I can retrieve it."

"But when I attempt it, it clenches yet tighter."

"Please, my dear, calm yourself."

Miss Anna turned another corner that came out of nowhere. For a second she believed herself to be walking on the ceiling, before the room abruptly righted itself. The base of her skull was pounding.

And then she saw a sight that filled her with unnameable horror.

For as another puckering portal dilated, and she stepped into an inner chamber, she saw Arabella hitching up her skirts, and Monsieur Clatoux reaching into her unmentionables with a monstrous instrument — a pair of tongs! Flanders House be damned! The den of iniquity was right here at Applethwaite!

Miss Anna screamed.

10

Nocturnes

Miss Arabella panicked and her clenched thighs immediately lost their hold on the meteorite, which landed on the floor of the spaceship with a metallic thud. She saw her sister through the dilated portal, screaming horrifically, her hands outstretched as if to ward off the very Prince of Darkness.

"Sister!" she cried out. "You must not carry on so! There is nothing remiss here! It is not as it seems!"

But Miss Anna was continuing to screech and wail. It was unlike her not to have a sarcastic riposte for everything she encountered, however scandalous; for her to carry on like an inebriated banshee was most disconcerting.

"I say, Monsieur!" Arabella said. "You really *must* do something."

"Indeed I must." Monsieur strode over to the opening in the wall and seized Anna's hands. He pulled her through the portal and into the inner room. "Calm yourself, Miss Anna!" he said, with such vehemence that Anna's caterwauling was stifled.

For Miss Anna stared first at Miss Arabella and then at the Monsieur, then back and forth a few more times. She was about to start carrying on again, but —

"Quiet!" Unable to control herself, Arabella stepped forward and slapped her sister resoundingly.

Anna did not speak, but tears sprang to her eyes. The sisters had had their share of battles, but usually avoided physical violence, preferring as their weapon of choice a decorous irony. Arabella immediately regretted it. But her sister's hysteria had to be silenced, or things would get out of hand.

"I'm sorry, sister," Arabella said. "But you *must* pull yourself together. If Monsieur Clatoux were not in imminent mortal danger, you would not have seen me in such an apparently compromising situation. Please hear the Monsieur out! You know very well that you and I — and indeed the entire standing of our household — hangs upon his good will — nay, his very survival."

Monsieur managed to escort Miss Anna to a kind of metallic ledge that protruded from the wall. It seemed to have just materialized; for the interior of the vessel had a knack of adjusting itself to accommodate its passengers. Miss Anna sat. The ledge shimmered and fluffed out, becoming more like a cushion. Arabella's sister leaned backward, dabbing at her eyes with a sleeve. "There had better be a dashed good reason for the spectacle I just witnessed," she said. "If my very own sister were ruined, how then should I bear it? I'm sure I should not care to live."

"Oh, stuff and nonsense," Arabella said. "It is all to help Monsieur to *telephone* home."

"Yes," Monsieur said, retrieving the meteorite from the floor. "It is true that your sister and I *did* purloin this celestial rock from your village hall, but it contains rare elements from beyond your world that I need to construct a device with which I can contact others of my kind."

"Heavens!" said Anna. "Other Frenchmen?"

"I think," Arabella said, "we need perhaps to let you in on our secret. You see, whereas all Frenchman are, by definition, aliens … it is not true that all aliens are Frenchmen."

"But … wogs begin at Calais."

"Sister!" Arabella said, more shocked at the use of this word than at any of her sister's blasphemies. "That is a shameful aphorism indeed. This is the nineteenth century! The notion of our English racial superiority has no place in the modern world … at least as far as the French are concerned."

"I suppose I … *am* a little old-fashioned," Miss Anna said. "After all, I don't read scientific books, as you do. Science — fiction — it's all rubbish."

"My dear Miss Anna," said Monsieur Clatoux. "Miss Arabella divined the truth the day I arrived. But you deserve to know this too. I am not, as it happens, actually from your world at all."

"Are you telling me you're … a ghost?"

"My dear Miss Anna — did you not touch my firm blue flesh? Did it seem discorporate to you?"

"Well … not as such."

Arabella said, "Monsieur. You must win her over. Perform one of your transubstantiation 'tricks' — or show her one of your extraordinary powers."

"Very well," said Monsieur Clatoux. "If you might allow me temporary custody of your sister, Miss Arabella, I shall show her a thing or two that will convince her. For while my ship is not yet ready to leap through time and space, I think I can expend enough energy for an instantaneous journey of some 1,733 miles."

"What!" Anna cried. "You will abduct me? Fie, Monsieur!"

"Trust me," said Monsieur Clatoux, his pointed ears quivering.

Miss Anna did not know *what* to think. Indeed, before she could actually think, the entire vessel began rumbling, and sparks of blue lightning started to dance from wall to wall in the chamber. A glowing, multicoloured cloud of scintillant dust-specks engulfed them all. She was too frightened to scream. Indeed, her throat was so raw from her previous exertions that she doubted she could produce much more than a strangulated squawk.

The rumbling became a roar. It was deafening. How could Monsieur act so calm? He was merely manipulating some objects that seemed to be painted in light and hanging in the air. Yet when he tapped this one and that, they shifted. She looked at her sister, who was watching, enthralled, in one hand grasping a rock which she recognized as having once been on exhibit in the village hall. So that part of the tale, at least, was true.

And suddenly, the ship was still, and silent.

"A rough ride, I'm afraid," said Monsieur, "but we are extremely low on dysprosium. Once I perform a little chromatography on the meteorite, we shall have more than enough."

"I don't understand," Miss Anna said. "We haven't actually *gone* anywhere, have we?"

"We have, in one sense, but not in another," said Monsieur. "We are still anchored in your apple orchard, but *that* coordinate is in the eleventh dimension. It's really very simple, or would be if your kind knew anything of string theory." He turned to Miss Arabella. "My dear, you must remain here. For, in the unlikely event that something should go wrong …"

"But I wish to see where we have come to!" said Arabella.

"If I survive, you shall have plenty of opportunity for that," said Monsieur. "And you must understand that this journey is for your sister's sake, to assuage *her* doubts. For you already know the truth."

He waved his arms and made a few mystic passes in the air. The shapes of light vanished, as did the sparkling vapours. Instead, there were three round knobs embedded in the wall.

"I have programmed everything you need," said Monsieur, "into these three buttons. I shall now take Miss Anna with me. Now, Miss Arabella, please remember what I shall tell you. We shall return within the hour. You will hear my voice reverberating from without the vessel, at which point you must push the *fuchsia* button. Should we not have returned by one hour from now, you will have to muster your courage and push the *primrose* button. For this will mean that all is lost, and that command will transport you and the ship back to Little Chiswick, leaving your sister and myself stranded. But you, at least, will be safe."

"There is a third button, Monsieur Clatoux."

"Ah, yes. The *cerulean* button. Push that if ever you need a cup of tea."

Alighting from the vessel, Miss Anna was helped down to the ground. She was secretly not displeased that her sister was forced to guard the ship and that she was embarking on an adventure with Monsieur, entirely unchaperoned.

It felt deliciously naughty, and she could almost comprehend how her sister might be tempted to go on such intrepid journeys ... such as entering the village hall with only a Frenchman for an escort! ... how exciting that must have been.

And now here she was, in a courtyard of what was clearly a palace; Monsieur was taking her by the arm, and total strangers were walking past, speaking gibberish — for it was not even French.

"Pray tell, Monsieur Clatoux. Where are we?"

"We are in an inner courtyard of the Imperial Palace of St. Petersburg," he said.

"Heavens!" Now she realized why she did not understand a word that was being spoken. "We're in Scotland!"

"My dear Miss Anna, Scotland is not a thousand miles away from Little Chiswick. But ... you will soon *hear* why we have come all the way to Russia."

Indeed, she did. For they had crossed the courtyard, and they were now in a huge hall, hung with splendid paintings, with ornate mouldings and a domed ceiling painted with a scene of the gods of Olympus. At the other end of the hall, there stood a pianoforte, and a man was playing.

It was music whose every note she had struggled through, music she knew intimately. That cascading scale — why, it had taxed her fingers for a month before she could even get the notes in the right order, but here it flew effortlessly from the fingers into the keys into the air. Each chord was perfectly placed. Each melismatic phrase was exquisitely turned, rising and falling like the ripple of a river.

Anna hardly dared to breathe, let alone move closer. But, led by Monsieur Clatoux, she approached the pianoforte. The closer she came, the more magical the sounds. When, at length, the nocturne ended, Miss Anna stood, silent, as though she had gazed through a window at paradise itself.

The man rose from the pianoforte and, seeing, the two of them, said, "Why, Nicolai! I haven't seen you in an age."

"I've been to my world," said Monsieur Clatoux. Then he said to Anna, "Here, I am known as Nicolai. It is an attempt to pronounce a different segment of my name from the one your family has distorted into *Clatoux.*" He turned to the gentleman musician and said, "John, might I presume to introduce Miss Dorrit?"

No wonder this man appeared to open up the gates of Heaven! He could only be the legendary John Field, the greatest composer of the age! And to hear the master perform his own compositions!

"I'm charmed, I'm sure, Mr. Field. For I am an immense admirer of your nocturnes."

"What a delight!" said Mr. Field. "An Englishwoman! How I have yearned to hear the dulcet tones of the English tongue from the lips of a member of the fairer sex!"

"Well, damn me to everlasting perdition!" Anna exclaimed, unable to control her excitement.

"Such words, from your lips, are as gall transmuted into honey," Mr. Field said. "I do love it when a woman blasphemes!"

"I knew you two would get along," said Monsieur Clatoux. "But we may not remain long. In less than an hour comes our apocolocyntosis."

"He means that you shall turn into pumpkins," said Mr. Field, laughing. "But I insist: you shall not leave until I have played for you my latest composition. For I too, have only a short time. I shall presently have to perform privately for His Imperial Majesty, Tsar Alexander of all the Russias. In less than an hour, the domestics of the palace will come to prepare the hall."

"A nocturne never before heard in Little Chiswick?" Anna said. "Can you teach it to me?"

"In an hour?"

"I beg you, sir." She knew she was being too forward, but being in the presence of her idol emboldened her.

And thus it was that Miss Anna received instruction from the world's greatest pianist, and committed a new, unpublished nocturne to memory. "I am sure I shall *murder* your masterpiece when I play it at the next soirée," she said.

"On the contrary," said Mr. Field, "the only better playing I heard was from nine-year old Fryderyk Szopen, a little Polish boy, whom I heard play for the Tsar when the court visited Warsaw. I told him to move to Paris, for he would be wasted on the Poles."

And then Mr. Field kissed her hand. Her very being thrilled with the touch of those lips! She trembled. Surely this was not something that could ever be permitted in Little Chiswick. But here, in this barbarous hinterland, in Russia, rules could be broken with impunity. Never had she felt more liberated.

It was with the greatest reluctance that Anna realized she must leave the presence of Mr. Field. *Tempus fugit* — the clock was ticking. They had but minutes to reach the ship. As they entered the courtyard, it began to snow. They started running. A guard saw them and shouted in Russian. They sprinted now, not an easy task in Miss Anna's voluminous clothes. The ship came in sight.

"Oh no!" said Monsieur. "Miss Arabella must have obeyed my instructions to the second!"

For the portal was closing. They leapt the last few steps and dived through the opening which closed with a puckering sound.

"I've lost my shoe!" Anna exclaimed, for it had become separated from her left foot in the lunge.

"At least," said Monsieur, "we shall not be pumpkinified today. Miss Arabella! The primrose knob!"

Miss Arabella was slouched on the ledge, arm outstretched, her finger lingering on the fuchsia button. The entire floor was littered with empty teacups. She had passed out.

"Is she alive?" Miss Anna started to shake her sister.

The Russian guard was banging on the outside wall.

"Are you sure it was tea?" said Miss Anna.

"Remind me to recalibrate that nutri-synthesizer," Monsieur mumbled as he pushed the primrose button himself.

11

Prudence and Prudery

It seemed as though very little time had passed before the day came for the Earl's ball. Anna and Arabella showed their anxiety in different ways. Anna took. to the pianoforte with renewed fortitude, battering at the keys with steely fingers, doubtless inspired by the example of Mr. Field. Arabella did nothing to prepare at all; instead, she embarked on an unlikely treasure-hunt with Monsieur, often borrowing the barouche and going, entirely unchaperoned, with him to the unlikeliest places.

The device was taking shape, and Arabella could see it was like nothing on Earth. There was a broken velocipede at its core, and it was attached to a beehive beneath a bell jar. A funnel was attached by a pipe to the bell jar, into which there dripped a fluid from the distillation of flower petals. The entire contraption resembled one of the monstrous machines of this new age, Arabella thought; she had seen an engraving of a spinning jenny before. But the addition of a retort, heated by a whale oil lamp, and some dangling, tinkling crystals, gave it an ancient look, like something from an alchemist's laboratory as well as a modern machine.

"This telephonic communication device," said Monsieur, "is close to completion. As soon as we can find a way to transport it to the London Mechanical Museum, I will summon my *mother ship,* and you shall be rid of me, for I have been a thankless burden."

"I pray you," Miss Arabella said, "do not consider yourself as such! You have brought amazement and wonder into our lives. I for one have seen such glimpses of other existences, other worlds, that I feel you have transformed my very being. You have made my sister into a quite different person as well; and as for my mother — while she may still imagine that you hail from France — she has been given a measure of hope in what would otherwise have been a dull, grey widowhood."

Monsieur seemed much moved by this outburst. Indeed, so passionate was Miss Arabella's utterance that she feared her corset might have cracked. Her hand flew to her left side, where the whalebone was weakest.

"I still have a few raw materials left to find," said Monsieur. "I hope I shall be able to locate them ... before my frail form falls victim to your world's oppressive gravity and toxic atmosphere."

Miss Arabella had not heard Monsieur Clatoux speak so disparagingly about her world. Trying to cheer him up, she said, "Tomorrow, at least, we will go to the ball. And you shall be able to study a few more of our curious ... as you call them ... *mating rituals*"

He sighed.

By four o'clock, Miss Arabella, along with her mother and sister, where already arriving at the stately residence of The Right   Honourable Tobias David Chrysostom George Mary Durham-St.Aubin-Borgnis, Ninth Earl of Little Chiswick and Viscount Blueborough.

And what a spectacle there was to behold! Past the chapel, which was the furthest Miss Arabella had penetrated into the estate, a broad, straight driveway was lined with mythological statues; they might be considered to be a bit shocking in their state of déshabillé, but nudity was not objectionable in antiquities.

"I'll have to avert my eyes," she heard her mother say as the barouche went forward (not the second-best, for *this* occasion) "as I'm sure such things are not meant for polite ladies to look upon." They passed a statue with a particularly prominent ... ah ... procreative organ.

"Do not worry, my dear sister," said the Reverend Bumbry. Arabella recognized most of the subjects, indeed, and found none of them inflaming. "That one we are just passing, for example ... that is David standing over the head of Goliath. Indeed, he's naked, but the subject is, after all, biblical."

"The one on the right," Arabella said, "I'm afraid is a little more distressing, Mama. It depicts the handsome youth Ganymede being ravished by Jupiter, disguised as an eagle."

"But how is that even possible?" said Mrs. Dorrit.

"You'd be surprised, my dear," said Mr. Bumbry, "at the contortions people will undergo for the sake of a few seconds of bliss."

"As a student of your world," Monsieur added,"It does amaze me that your species has so frequently risked life and limb, nay, even the fate of entire nations and empires, on the expectation of unburdening oneself of a thimbleful of white fluid."

"I have *no* idea what you mean," said Mrs. Dorrit.

"Oh, she does, Monsieur," said Miss Arabella. "She has, after all, had two children."

"I most certainly do *not*," Mrs. Dorrit said, though Arabella suspected that her mother knew exactly what was being discussed. After all, even *she* knew how babies were made. It was something to do with the insertion of a firm, cyclindrical device. Every man, she had heard, carried such a thing on his person.

But now all talk was stilled, for they had reached the sweeping double stairway that led to the front door of the manse. The portal was wide open and the light that shone forth was dazzling — surely they had used up the blubber of an entire whale to light the interior! The sun was still in the sky, yet the rectangle of light from the open entrance made even the daylight pale!

And the music that issued forth! This was no quartet, but a symphony, playing tunes from the most fashionable operas, such as *Maometto Secondo* and *La Schiava in*

Baghdad! Music Miss Arabella had never listened to in the flesh, for she had but heard her sister struggle through transcriptions written for the pianoforte.

As they stepped down and stood in the entrance, where a grand foyer with yet another sweeping double stairway could be seen, all in marble, they saw no people, except for the odd liveried servant with a tray. Huge paintings were displayed, including a portrait of that most wicked Catholic queen, Queen Mary and her Spanish husband. There was also a mythological painting showing Jupiter accosting various nymphs and goddesses in the form of a bear, a bull, a swan, and a shower of gold.

The sound of the music was louder now and it issued from a ballroom to the right. Leaving their pelisses with a footman, who carried them to some inner cloakroom, the party stepped into the ballroom just as the orchestra finished a musical introduction.

At that moment, a woman began to sing. Arabella recognized the air immediately; it was from *Maometto* indeed, and was the plaintive and haunting "*Ah! In vain I call for sweet oblivion!*" which she had seen in Anna's pianoforte transcription book. At one end of the hall was a full-sized concert stage, and the woman, in a splendid gown of blue silk, commanded so much attention that there was scarcely a whisper in the room, though it was filled with the cream of ton society. Arabella could see that Anna, too, was entranced. This singer could be none other than the legendary Signora Sforzando, the shining star of the Royal Opera, and it was something only the Earl could have accomplished, the miracle of plucking this diva from the lofty stage of Covent Garden to perform in a private hall in Little Chiswick!

Anna and the Frenchman were utterly ensorcelled by the signora's limpid melismas.

So Arabella was all the more nonplussed when her mother began to speak in stentorian tones. "I told you, Mr. Bumbry, those Catholics have no shame! Imagining sullying the pristine purity of this palace with the presence of … an *actress!*"

Although Mrs. Dorrit had used the word *actress*, Miss Arabella was sure that she had actually intended a word somewhat more alliterative than that, only she had been unable to let it pass her lips.

"Oh shush, sister!" said Mr. Bumbry. Others, too, turned around to stare at the Dorrits. "She is a veritable nightingale."

"But we do not allow *actresses* in good society!" said Mrs. Dorrit.

"Not *every* actress is …a harlot," said Mr. Bumbry.

At that moment, Signora Sforzando attacked a high D with such ear-splitting clarity that the entire audience's jaws dropped as one.

All jaws, that is, except Mrs. Dorrit's. "I've heard enough," she said, taking a daughter in each hand, and propelling them towards the door. Mr. Bumbry did not move, and as for Monsieur, he was as entranced as the rest of the throng.

The top D was still going on when they stepped into the hall—

And Arabella practically walked right into the arms of the Right Honourable Earl of Little Chiswick. He was just as charming — and twice as rakish — as he had been in their previous encounter.

"Heavens!" he murmured. "My dear Arabella! I knew that you found me of some interest, but I hardly thought you would fling yourself into my arms at the next opportunity!"

"You *are* a devil, Your Lordship!" said Arabella.

"And like Lucifer, I intend to light up your life."

Mrs. Dorrit shrieked at him, "How dare you accost my daughter so, you unprincipled papist!"

"Not in His Lordship's house!" said Mr. Bumbry, emerging from the ballroom. "I have set my righteous prejudice at popery in order to allow your daughters the opportunity for advancement! I have done this for your sake, to the profound impoverishment of my immortal soul. If I can control myself, Madam, so can you!"

Mrs. Dorrit silenced herself in mid-gurgle.

"Your Lordship," she said, and curtsied.

"Ah," said His Lordship. "I'm delighted to see that you are cognisant of my station in life. Please, enjoy my little gathering. As you can see, I have spared no expense; Signora Sforzando normally sings in private for no one except His Majesty, who, as you know loves nothing better than to spend his time amongst songbirds, be they human or avian."

"Mother," said Arabella in Mrs. Dorrit's ear, "if His Majesty himself receives her, she's probably *not* a pr—"

"Don't say it," said Mrs. Dorrit. "One foul-mouthed daughter is enough."

At that moment, the Signora finally came off the top D, which she had sustained for nigh on a full minute. Applause broke out before the orchestra could play its final ritornello.

It was a great relief, Arabella thought, that only her family, and the Earl, were in this hallway, unless you were to count the footmen. She could have died of embarrassment. She could see that her mother was deeply torn between propriety and prudence. "We've got a very interesting Frenchman," she said, hoping to change the subject. "Would you like to see him?"

"Indeed I would," said the Earl. "And I shall, once the signora's divertissement is done. At that time, the quadrilles will be starting, and I shall also claim the first dance of the evening, which is what your daughter promised me."

"My daughter — promised — you—" Mrs. Dorrit spluttered, staring at her daughter with simultaneous admiration and disapproval. Mr. Bumbry raised an eyebrow.

"I pray you," said the Earl, "let me borrow your daughter for a few moments. I would like to show her the garden. It is a fine example of the Tudor invention, a "knot garden," made in the form of a labyrinth of hedges. We shall not be long, and there will be plenty of my liveried staff hovering in the background, so you need fear nothing improper, Mrs. Dorrit."

With those words — as a man unused to being refused any request, presumably — His Lordship took Arabella boldly by the right arm and whisked her away in the direction of the double stairwell, beneath which a French window led to the private grounds of the estate, heedless of the turmoil he had left in his wake.

12

Minuet and Madness

As she watched His Lordship exit the foyer with her daughter on his arm, Mrs. Dorrit was compelled to make a complete reassessment of all she had ever professed and held dear. For it was clear that the Earl was taken with Arabella. Either that, or he considered himself so exalted as to be able to take any liberty with any innocent girl. Surely even a Catholic would not stoop to that! He was, after all, an Earl … and the dream of having a Countess for a daughter seemed suddenly to be not implausible.

Taking courage, she took Mr. Bumbry's arm and said, "Lead the charge, dear brother! With the good Lord on our side, we shall defeat them all — papists, beings from other worlds, Frenchmen — present company excepted — and all the gossips and naysayers of this ton!"

"Speaking of present company—" said Mr. Bumbry.

Monsieur Clatoux was indeed at the centre of what looked like an adoring throng. He was regaling them with stories about ... *France.*

"No, indeed," he was saying, "we do not *all* have blue skins; some of us are purple. This is due to copper or manganese being the central atom of the oxidizing catalyst in our cells, you see, much as your people have red blood because of the iron in haemoglobin, and plants have green chlorophyll. So, to answer your question, we have no little green men in our world."

Mrs. Dorrit saw at once that while the elite of Little Chiswick were fascinated, they were also baffled. Monsieur was amusing them with what seemed like extravagant and fantastical fictions. He was entertaining, in the manner of a court jester, or even a sort of noble savage. She felt demeaned on his behalf, yet Monsieur did not seem to mind; indeed, he endured their supercilious queries with grace. *I do admire him,* she realized. Unbidden, her first vision of him, like a blue Adam in an English Eden, floated up into her consciousness and she tried to brush it aside, for mingled with that image was also a remembrance of her late husband, reaching for her in their marital bower ... I am *such* a sinner! she thought. But the thought was delicious, rather than bitter. *Heavens! I am drawn to him! Or is it merely that the years of being deprived of a husband make me attracted to any male who would even give me the time of day — even a Frenchman?*

Mrs. Dorrit surveyed the guests with interest — especially since thinking of the others prevented her from worrying about whether Arabella was off somewhere being debauched.

Presently, one the matrons, Mrs. Gotham-Clarke, who had three ungainly but marriageable daughters named Edna, Edwina, and Evangelina, asked Monsieur, "And what are the dances like in France? How are the quadrilles? The minuets?"

Monsieur looked across at Mrs. Dorrit. She could see from his eyes that he needed her help, for entertaining though his stories were, she knew that he could not improvise a French dance convincingly, for dancing was perhaps the only accomplishment in which *every* young woman was schooled — and he might be caught out!

At that moment, Signora Sforzando, who had been singing a lively cabaletta, finished with a virtuoso cadenza to thunderous applause and left the stage. The orchestra struck up a solemn minuet.

Mrs. Dorrit, coming to the rescue, took Monsieur Clatoux by the hand and said, "Thank you for inviting me to be your partner in demonstrating the new French variant of the minuet." With a forwardness she did not know she had, she steered Monsieur towards the centre of the dance floor, whispering, "Just do what I do! Any oddities will doubtless will be imputed to your Frenchness!"

With that, she curtsied — and so did Monsieur. She took a step to the right — and so did Monsieur. "No, no, Monsieur Clatoux! Your *other* right! *Mirror* me! Else we will end up on opposite sides of the ballroom!"

She was rusty, she knew, but she had once been accomplished at the art; certainly, her terpsichorean skills had drawn her late husband's attention. But as she stepped elegantly, twice forward, twice to the left, it became apparent that Monsieur had two left feet … and two left arms as well. He moved awkwardly, and presently got himself quite tangled up; she swept behind him, spinning him so as to untwist his elbows and knees which had somehow managed to get into a knot. The guests applauded.

And then, they were all doing it too! She could see some of the most dignified women of the ton making fools of themselves, thinking this the latest French fashion!

"This is exhilarating!" cried Mrs. Gotham-Clarke, who was dancing with a rather embarrassed-looking twelve-year-old, perhaps some cousin of the Chuzzlewits and thus of Mrs. Dorrit as well.

"Splendid! Splendid!" opined the seductive Miss Talliaferro, as one of the Farthingale brothers dragged her into the crowd of dancers.

Monsieur's ineptitude was causing chaos, for the minuet is nothing if not an *orderly* affair, the steps most carefully adhered to. Yet he did nothing of the kind. Sometimes he pointed a toe behind in a kind of crooked arabesque. Sometimes he hopped like a frog. The others loved it, and began hopping as well.

"Monsieur," Mrs. Dorrit gasped, as she tried to lead him back to a more civilised posture, "You are rendering me quite out of breath; pray do not be so energetic!"

In response, Monsieur Clatoux put his arm out to steady her, clasping her waist in a most unseemly fashion. Immediately, the other couples began to do it too. As Mrs. Dorrit attempted to wriggle free, Monsieur Clatoux moved with her, doubtless concerned that she might swoon, especially as, at her age, she was less able to cope with her corset. She found herself whirling through the ballroom, leading a dozen couples in a dizzying spin, like a top losing steam. The others, being younger and having perhaps been to more balls, imitated their every action adeptly, missing nary a beat.

"Mother!" cried the twelve-year-old to Mrs. Gotham-Clarke. "You never told me these grown-up affairs were such fun!"

"Be silent, Marmaduke!" said Mrs. Gotham-Clarke, as her son spun her round and round. "I shall expire!"

"My dear Monsieur Clatoux," said Mrs. Dorrit. "This is no stately minuet. This is the scandalous *waltz*, that newfangled invention from Germany!"

Gasping for air, she forced Monsieur to a halt. Immediately, all the other dancers settled back into the graceful, pre-choreographed motions of the minuet.

"Dear me! My throat is *utterly* dry!" she said, leading Monsieur towards a footman, who was approaching them with a tray of champagne flutes. Quickly she downed an entire glass, and managed to seize a second before the servant had wandered too far off.

"Air!" she said. "Air!"

Monsieur Clatoux escorted her to the foyer, though not before Mrs. Dorrit had been able to deposit her second flute and catch a third from another footman. The front door was still open to receive any latecomers, and a welcome breeze wafted in. She stood there, looking at the outside world, her mind a little addled by having consumed two glasses of champagne in short order. They stood in the brilliant light of gas and whale oil, but through that portal, the night beckoned. There was moonlight on the pathway, and the starlight shone soft and sensuous over the avenue lined with statues and trees. Those nude men in marble seemed far less shocking now. Nay, the pearly glow of the marble, set against the deep shadows of the trees, made her long for ... *something*. She could not put a name to it. These were feelings she had never had with the late Mr. Dorrit.

"Why, my dear Mrs. Dorrit," said Monsieur Clatoux. "Your mood has changed entirely. Indeed, the air is laced with certain pheromones that appear to be emanating from various crevices of your body."

"What *ever* are you saying, Monsieur?" said Mrs. Dorrit, her speech beginning to slur. She was feeling faint indeed, and giddy, and was slowly slumping backwards into his arms.

"I am emboldened to ask you, Madam, whether, when we return to the cottage tonight ... you would care to mate?"

13

Quandary and Quadrille

And where was Miss Anna while these emotional tempests raged in the hearts of the other Dorrit women? Anna really saw little of interest in the ballroom. Every bachelor who might be remotely eligible was already queuing up for a woman with greater prospects than herself. Most, in fact, were trying to speak either to one of the wealthy Gotham-Clarke sisters, the elder being reckoned the easiest to deal with, or the seductive Miss Taliaferro, whose father had acquired vast tobacco holdings in Virginia. The grotesque Lady Sanditon had a following as well, for she came with aristocratic connections and the hope of social advancement.

Anna could see, too, that her mother, and Monsieur, were performing a bizarre parody of a minuet, and that some of the other guests were gyrating in imitation. "Oh, dear!" she said to her uncle. "Mama has become the belle of the ball — or perhaps *la bête*," she added ruefully as the couple executed a move halfway between an arabesque and a somersault.

"Do you wish to dance, my dear?" said Mr. Bumbry. "Although perhaps you should not deem it terribly exciting to be seen minueting with a vicar."

"I shall wander about," Anna said, "and, who knows, find a potential husband in the midst of this assemblage of beaux."

And wander about she did. She had been excited about coming here; and hearing a live orchestra, not to mention the famed Signora Sforzando, had been a thrill, but she was less enamoured of the predatory game that was now afoot. *Game*, indeed, was what it was ... what *all the women* were ... for she and the rest had become foxes in a hunt, with the gentlemen sniffing about them like bloodhounds.

The orchestra commenced a quadrille, and couples were shuffling now. One of the Farthingale boys, the pockmarked Andrew, was loping in Anna's direction, and she panicked.

"Uncle, I *must* take the air for a moment," she said, rushing from the room via the nearest door. This led to a narrow passageway. It must be part of the honeycomb of secret ways for the servants to get where they were summoned as quickly as possible. It was unlit, and she fumbled about for a moment before finding another doorknob. Pushing it open, she found herself in a dimly lit chamber.

A single candelabrum, its candles almost spent, flickered. Here and there, velvet drapes were hung. "There must a window somewhere," Anna murmured, drawing the first of the curtains. But it was a painting, not a window. She was staring at a beautiful woman, exquisitely painted, her eyes and lips wide open in some kind of transcendent ecstasy. Curiously, Miss Anna drew the curtains a little more. Why, the woman was completely naked! And rearing up above her, there was naked man. She assumed it was a man. But if it was, his nether regions sported an enormous, cigar-shaped fleshy spike that sprang from a veritable forest of hair, and beneath it dangled twin cylindrical sacks of wrinkled, sagging skin.

She screamed.

The room became a little brighter. She spun around. There was a man in the chamber! He had come in with a whale oil lamp, whilst she had been screaming.

"Cousin!" he said. "Whatever are you doing here?"

"I was … admiring the art," said Miss Anna weakly.

She was relieved that the man was none other than Lord Chuzzlewit; propriety was still intact. "Are you lost? Perhaps you are searching for the … ah … *petite chambre?*"

"Indeed," said Anna, "I was."

"I shall escort you."

"What is this place?"

"Oh, it is the *sanctum sanctorum,* I'm afraid. It's where the gentlemen withdraw after dinner. Women are not allowed, I'm afraid, except for the occasional servant. But, I am so glad you have an eye for the art. That painting you've been looking at, is in fact, quite old; it is called *Original Sin.*"

"But the man's … ah … nether proboscis …"

"Realistic, isn't it?"

"Cousin, it is nothing like those classical statues that grace the driveway into Flanders House.   It is ... *monstrous.*"

"Of course, dear cousin," said Lord Chuzzlewit. "Your delicate sensibilities. You have probably never laid eyes upon a male member in its full, stalwart glory, when aroused by a beautiful woman such as yourself."

"I most certainly have not!"

"Alas, you have had the misfortune of being born a member of the weaker sex. Proper ladies have no inkling of what awaits them, whereas young men have plenty of opportunities to, ah, practise the art of love, as they may available themselves of ladies of the night or even those trollops that lurk in dark alleys, even here in Little Chiswick."

Miss Anna gazed at the painting once more and could see now that it was indeed a kind of representation of the Garden of Eden. For not only were there a man and a woman, engaged in some mysterious activity, but in the background there were various animals, including a lion, a lamb, and a serpent, and a quince dangled, glistening, from a tree-branch above them. There was nary a fig leaf in sight, though, and she could not imagine such a painting in a church, even a Roman Catholic one.

"This boudoir has many fine works. I was hoping to take a look, as I am rarely vouchsafed an invitation to Flanders House. The last Earl was very much a connoisseur of the arts, especially those in which the artist dared to ... take a few risks. This one, for instance ..." He drew aside another curtain. *"Leda penetrated by the Swan."*

A beautiful woman, again naked, was emerging from a pool of water. The swan was the same size as she. The swan's head was buried neck-deep in the nymph's ... Anna looked away. She had never known such art was possible. "Here's one of the Earl's most splendid acquisitions — a Caravaggio. The third Earl received it as a gift from Cardinal Del Monte himself, almost two centuries ago! It is called the *Rape of Ganymede.*"

Anna gasped. For just as in the *Leda,* there was a gigantic bird, an eagle this time, making free with the helpless, unclothed form of a human being. Only this one was male, and the location of the eagle's head was ... not a location Anna had imagined to be anatomically possible.

"Notice the use of chiaroscuro," said Lord Chuzzlewit.

She had indeed noticed. It was the chiaroscuro, in fact, that rendered what should have been the most provocative part of the painting into deepest shadow, salvaging at least a modicum of propriety.

So this was the secret life of men, in those times and places where their wives and daughters were forbidden to intrude. Tobacco, brandy, and paintings of wanton licentiousness! Miss Anna longed to take refuge in one of John Field's elegant nocturnes. Surely musicians did not need to have lewd thoughts, since their heads were clearly in the clouds, drinking in the Apollonian joys of the divine.

"But come, my dear cousin," said Lord Chuzzlewit. "I must show you to the *petite chambre,* and I can hear a second quadrille starting up. I hope you will join me for at least one dance."

Dazed, Anna followed him out into the corridor. His Lordship was being unusually friendly. It must have been because she had played the pianoforte at his soirée. Or, perhaps, meeting by happenstance in the room with the immoral paintings, the two of them now shared a secret, one they could not divulge to anyone else.

I shan't even tell Mama, she thought.

14

Mayhem and Majesty

Miss Arabella, having been rather smoothly spirited away from the ballroom by an Earl who was not used to hearing the word *no*, found herself at the bowered entrance to a secret garden, with His Lordship fidgeting with a padlock!

"Your Lordship —" she began.

"I pray you, call me David."

"I hope you do not have anything underhanded in mind, Your Lordship."

"You don't like the name David? Call me Toby, then," said the Right Honourable Tobias David Chrysostom George Mary Durham-St.Aubin-Borgnis, Ninth Earl of Little Chiswick and Viscount Blueborough. "I haven't got anything underhanded planned. Though perhaps I do entertain fantasies of having my hands *under* those overwrought garments of yours."

"I should slap you, my Lord, for giving voice to such an unwholesome sentiment."

"Do, pray."

Arabella raised her right hand and prepared to strike a resounding blow against the tyranny of the male sex, but he started laughing, and she could not help laughing herself. This game seemed so ridiculous. Indeed, in a moment they were giggling like children.

"In truth, Your Lordship," she said, "I do not much enjoy this game that society makes us play. I'd much rather spend time with my books, and in the pursuit of learning. But you already knew this."

"Call me George?" said the Earl of Little Chiswick.

She laughed again. "You are blessed with a multitude of names! How ever do you remember them all?"

"You may call me by any name you wish, my dear, but avoid Chrysostom — only my mother ever dared call me that."

The music from within the manse played softly here, blending with the whisper of the wind and the occasional cry of a nightingale. The sky was cloudless. "If we stand here long enough," Arabella said, "Orion will rise." She wondered which of the stars was the home of Monsieur Clatoux.

"Not yet," the Earl said. "We would have to stand here until three of the clock, and my guests will have danced themselves into a stupor."

"Oh!" said Miss Arabella. "You know of the constellations!"

"My dear Miss Arabella," said the Earl, "imagine, if you will, Virginia. My small tobacco farm … vaster than anything possible in these isles … not a human being for miles around, save the slaves. The summer nights there are sweltering … you cannot imagine the heat and the moisture, though I think the Indies are hotter still. One stands on the porch with only the stars for company. They become one's friends. Orion, I love well, particularly Betelgeuse, ruddy as … your cheeks, Miss Arabella!"

"I must admit, my Lord, that was elegantly turned."

"Let me show you the Knot Garden. That was why I invited you out here, was it not?"

"I wonder if I should proceed any further. At least here, close to the door, I can quickly run back inside and no one will know we were ever alone together."

"Tongues will not wag," said the Earl. "Not in my house, at any rate."

"But they wag already, my Lord," said Arabella. "I grew up on tall tales of your exploits!"

"Then nothing I say or do will surprise you," he said. He opened the gate and led her inside.

The Knot Garden was magical. The maze, walled by hedges, spread out in every direction. She could not help being fascinated as the Earl led the way. There were turns, false entrances, abrupt dead-ends, and in the pale light the walls had a silvery shimmer, as though touched with fairy dust.

"The garden was designed by the third Earl of Little Chiswick," the Earl told her. "They were good times for my family. Bloody Queen Mary was burning protestants at the stake, and my ancestor managed to acquire several of their estates."

"That's certainly a divergent view of history," Miss Arabella said.

"Since then, we've been persecuted quite a bit," said the Earl. "I can't even take my proper seat in the House of Lords. There are fewer than a dozen Catholic peers. Why, twenty years ago, I could not attend mass in a church — only in my private chapel! But America ... oh, how free the air was! The vastness, the openness, the limitless possibilities! I've made and lost three fortunes there! I feel no compunction about participating in trade, in mercantile pursuits ... I feel the equal of every blacksmith, every soldier of fortune ... universal brotherhood."

"Even slaves?" said Arabella.

"Well, not the slaves, of course," he said.

"Yet you possessed ... a few hundred of them, on that tobacco plantation of yours?" Arabella had never seen an African up close. "Are they as brutish as they say?"

"Oh ... as they say ..." the Earl paused. He was remembering something. "If I said this to another landowner, he might think me mad. But they are not as barbaric as we would like to believe. In those lonely, endless days, I heard their stories. They, too, have legends of kings and princes, and gods as varied and colourful as the ancients, even if we have compelled them to appear to be Christians."

"If once you thought of them as human, you might question their enslavement," Miss Arabella said.

"You are more than a tantalizing morsel," said the Earl. "I do believe you might have a brain."

"And if you thought of women as other than 'tantalizing morsels,'" she went on, "you might question our subservience!"

"Such morsels are, indeed, food for thought."

Much to her own surprise, Miss Arabella realized that she rather liked the Earl. He actually appreciated her, in a strange way; and his own honesty about his predatory ways was in a sense endearing. She knew, however, that she was in perilous shoals.

Especially since the conversation had been so entertaining, she had not really counted the twists and turns of the labyrinth. She would not be able to extricate herself, should the Earl attempt to … ravish her. "Where are the, ah, liveried staff, the ones you said would be hovering in the background to ensure that I am not compromised?"

They turned a corner.

They had reached a kind of clearing; at its centre there was an open wooden structure with a roof, and in the middle, a life-sized wooden statue of a nude woman. An expressionless face, yet endowed with a capacious bosom and steatopygous hips. "That is my Venus," he said. "Plucked from a ruined city somewhere in the Territories of the Ottomans. I don't know if she's Greek, or Babylonian, or Indian." A lone torch lit up her blank eyes.

"Astonishing," Arabella said.

"Shall we worship?" said the Earl, and, without warning, seized her by the shoulders, drawing her into an embrace which, while she had not invited it, was not as unpleasant as she had thought it might be. Still, she had better put an end to it, she thought.

"Your Lordship!" she murmured, as she observed, with

some alarm, the increasing propinquity of his lips. "Should you not look in on your guests? Surely you are already missed!"

"My dear, dear, Arabella! We shall return in a minute, but surely you cannot deny me a fleeting taste of those honeyed —"

"*Chrysostom!* Stop this behaviour at once!"

It worked! Using *that name* had made the Earl think of his mother, squashing his romantic urges. She twisted free of his embrace. Wildly, she looked about, but could see no exit.

"You'll never get out of my Knot Garden!" the Earl said, recovering his bonhomie.

"Oh, but I shall," Arabella said grimly. "Have you not heard of how Alexander the Great solved the Gordian Knot?"

Screwing up all her strength, Arabella charged at the nearest hedge. She tore through the foliage. She crossed the path and crashed through the next hedge, and the next —

"You're destroying a four-hundred-year-old work of art!" the Earl screamed, as Arabella thrashed her way through to the outside, leaving an Arabella-shaped tunnel in her wake.

She was out. She saw the back terrace, the lights inside the house. The Earl had not followed through the opening she had ripped out of the bushes — presumably, he actually knew the proper way out — but in moments he emerged from the garden gate. Miss Arabella ran for dear life, pushing open the door of the manse just as the Earl managed to catch up with her, huffing and puffing —

At that very moment, as they stepped into the foyer, a panel in the wall behind the stairs popped open, and Lord Chuzzlewit emerged with Miss Anna. Anna appeared to be adjusting her clothing, and Lord Chuzzlewit seemed quite nonplussed to see Miss Arabella with the Earl.

"What on Earth have you done with my sister?" Arabella shrieked.

"Nothing," Anna said. "He was showing me the short cut to the *petite chambre.*"

The two sisters looked at each other — and then across the foyer, where Monsieur Clatoux, who had actually *removed his jacket*, appeared to be making free with Mrs. Dorrit, who swayed hither and thither while a footman stood by, with an entire tray of empty champagne flutes.

"Monsieur! What on Earth are you doing with my mother?" Anna screamed.

"Put that jacket on at once!" cried Arabella. "You're half naked!"

"Heavens!" the Earl exclaimed. He pulled a pistol from his jacket.

Now all three of the ladies were screaming, and the Earl, the Baron, and the alien were all jabbering at once.

The front door was flung open.

A personage stood in the doorway.

Shocked, everyone stopped shrieking all at once. There was dead silence.

Then the Earl broke out in a broad grin. "*Sapperment!*" he said, "*Tante Charlotte! Was für eine Ehre, daß Eure Majestät angekommen seid!*"

"*Chrystostom, mein Schatz!*" said the personage.

Who would call the Earl of Little Chiswick "Chrysostom,

darling?" Surely not his mother, for she had passed away. Only one person would say such a thing, *in German*, and be referred to by the Earl as "Auntie Charlotte."

Disbelieving, the women curtsied all the way to the floor and Lord Chuzzlewit bowed, practically folding himself in two. Monsieur Clatoux, having no clue who this was, backed away and observed the scene quietly.

In her sixties, the personage had a wig that added a good eight inches to her already impressive height. Her dress, in primrose-coloured silk, billowed about her like a massive tent. She was attended by a black page-boy, who had helped her across the threshold.

Gazing fixedly at Monsieur, she said, "Zo, dis is de notorious Frenchman de whole country is shpeaking off?"

"Might I introduce my third cousin once removed, Charlotte von Mecklenberg-Strelitz, Electress of Hanover?" said the Earl of Little Chiswick.

It would have been gilding the lily for him to add: *Queen of England.*

15

Shirtless in Flanders

"But why, pray," the Queen continued, "does Our French friend appear in dis manner, *sans chemise?"*

Mrs. Dorrit had to improvise an excuse, as it were, on the fly. For it was true that upon asking her whether she wanted to "mate," Monsieur had allowed his upper garments to begin to slip down his shoulders, and while it was in fact only his jacket that lay in a heap on the floor, his shirt, too, was half off. What a specimen! Mrs. Dorrit attempted to suppress the powerful emotions she felt at viewing his unclothed form, but she could not; instead, she tried to dredge up some sense of moral discomfiture.

Could he not have waited until they returned home before exhibiting such ... exhibitionism? she thought. Yet she had to admit that his pure, smooth, cerulean skin, rippling in the candlelight, was more alluring that it had any right to be.

And Her Majesty herself was not immune to its charms; or was it the maddeningly sensual scent that wafted from his body? The Queen was not reacting to Monsieur's savage state of déshabillé with quite the opprobrium expected from a person of such an exalted station. Indeed, she was smiling … nay, giggling like a schoolgirl.

"Mon cher cousin!" she said to the Earl, and it seemed to Mrs. Dorrit that the royal families of Europe all spoke in a kind of macaronic dialect in which their mother tongue was combined with the language of the country over which they ruled, with a liberal sprinkling of French. "Your Frenchman is delightful! And wonderfully free from de strictures of our civilization, *nicht wahr?* In de forty years dat We've been visiting Flanders House, We haff *never* seen a shirtless man in de foyer before! Oh, deliciously *méchant!"*

"Deepest apologies, Your Majesty," Mrs. Dorrit said. "Monsieur was merely showing me —" she floundered for an explanation —

"My … epidermal condition, Your Majesty," said Monsieur. "Since my visit to your country, so many strangers have enquired whether my blue coloration extends beyond my face and hands. I decided to satisfy their curiosity … by uncovering myself."

"Mon Dieu! Like circus animal!"

"Excuse him, Your Majesty," said Mrs. Dorrit. "He really knows no better."

"Let him show Us," said the Queen. "We would very much enjoy to see dis skin disease."

"But — to bare himself in front of a Queen —" Mrs. Dorrit said.

"As you say, he knows no better."

"Indeed, ma'am," said Monsieur, "I know no better. Where I come from we have nothing like your system of social interactions."

"How quaint!" said the Queen. "So you will disrobe?"

"Pray do not fret, ladies," said the Earl. "My aunt belongs in the most rarefied of circles; middle-class morality has no place amongst those anointed to rule over others."

The Earl called to some footmen and told them to block the door from the foyer to the ballroom. Music continued to play within, and they could hear laughter, conversation, and the clink of champagne flutes.

Other footmen approached with candelabra and oil lamps, and, holding them up, formed a circle. It was true, Mrs. Dorrit reflected, that the lives of the highest aristocracy were nothing like those of the minor landed gentry, and their view of morality far more fluid than the kind of thing Mr. Bumbry preached about on Sundays. Indeed, it was a good thing Mr. Bumbry was inside the ballroom.

It seemed that no one had any inkling that she herself might, but for the Queen's arrival, been ravished, and not that unwillingly, either. She had barely escaped the proverbial fate worse than death ... and was not entirely happy to have escaped.

As for the Earl rushing in in hot pursuit of one daughter, and Lord Chuzzlewit emerging from a secret entrance in the wall with the other, all of these things were at least things she had imagined ... on the frequent occasions when she imagined the worst for her daughters.

Yet the idea of Monsieur Clatoux revealing, with no

more shame than a baboon in the zoological gardens, the entirety of his beautifully wrought, perfectly-muscled, glistening body to no less a figure than the Queen of England was a conceit far beyond these tawdry imaginings. It was a depravity of epic proportions.

Monsieur's shirt slid to the floor. The women gasped, and even the two peers looked askance. While Mrs. Dorrit had endeavoured to forget her first sight of the Monsieur's emergence from the spaceship, what little she remembered suggested that he might have made a few improvements to his human physique. His skin was utterly without blemish — and the blue sheen was almost metallic, giving the hard outlines of his stomach muscles an almost machine-like perfection.

Monsieur stood in the pool of light, flexing his arms and assuming various statuesque positions. His hair seemed to have a life of its own, whipping this way and that in a wind that none could feel. He was, in a word, beautiful.

"Splendid," said Her Majesty. "But ... is dere not more?"

"Aunt Charlotte!" the Earl murmured, impressed.

Mrs. Dorrit was doubly thankful that her brother was not in the room, for surely this level of impropriety was even worse than could even be imagined of Catholics.

Swift to obey the royal command, Monsieur Clatoux undid his fly-buttons and allowed his trousers to drop, revealing a fine pair of thighs. And —

Suffice it to say that Monsieur Clatoux had definitely made a few small changes.

Or *big* changes, depending on one's point of view.

"Oh!" the Queen exclaimed. *"Wie ein Pferd!"*

Miss Arabella said to the Earl of Little Chiswick, "Your

Lordship, did Her Majesty just compare Monsieur to a horse?"

"Wahrlich ein Tannenbaum!" the Queen rhapsodized.

"Did she just call *that* a … Christmas tree?" Arabella said.

"She's got Christmas trees on the brain," said Anna. "Remember, it was she who introduced them to this country!"

"My dear Aunt Charlotte," he said, ignoring her, "I think Monsieur had better cover himself, before we are all blinded by this spectacle."

"Ja, ja," said the Queen. "But now, duty calls. We better join dis *verdammte* Ball."

Monsieur was now fully dressed again, almost by magic.

"And, Monsieur Clatoux," Her Majesty continued, "as you may deem it too forward to request it of a Queen, so We shall reply to de unspoken question. You may indeed have de honour of de first dance. Let it be a *German* dance!"

The Earl commanded that the door to the ballroom be flung open and that the footmen step aside.

"Tell the orchestra to strike up a waltz!" he commanded.

16

Harp and Hierarchy

Mrs. Dorrit felt a twinge of ... *je ne sais quoi* ... as Her Majesty seized Monsieur's hand and dragged him into the ballroom. Bows and curtsied ran around the hall like ocean waves, and the orchestra paused in mid-waltz to play a perfunctory rendition of *Heil Dir, Hannover*, which happens to have the same tune as *God Save the King*.

"Rather convenient for the sovereign and his queen, isn't it?" Miss Anna whispered to her mother. "They only have to play one anthem."

The Earl was lustily singing the words in German, and a few of the crowd were joining in in English.

"Why," said Mrs. Dorrit, "he actually knows it in German."

Arabella said, "He spent some years with the Mecklenberg-Strelitzes as a I child, as I've read. Apparently he father was fleeing religious persecution."

"Persecution?" Anna said. "I'd heard it was creditors."

"Debt collection is practised with great zeal when the debtors are of an offending faith," Mrs. Dorrit opined.

The anthem ended and segued into a waltz, and Her Majesty was sweeping Monsieur across the floor, practically taking the lead in this most scandalous of dances.

"Look at them whirl!" Arabella cried.

"She's agile for an septuagenarian, my Tante Charlotte," said the Earl of Little Chiswick. "My dear Arabella, pray join me."

"What! After you chasing me through the Knot Garden?" she said.

Mrs. Dorrit, sensing an opportunity, said, "My dear, this room is full of people; you are unlikely to be compromised if you don't go wandering off again."

She watched her daughter and the Earl merge into the throng. She wondered what they had been doing out in the garden by themselves, but they had clearly not provoked any talk, since no one had seen them. It was entirely possible that her bluestocking daughter might yet capture a prize.

As they waltzed, Miss Arabella said, "I've a mind to slap you right here in public."

"Heavens!" said the Earl. "You're as free-spirited as an American!"

"When you started to talk of the stars, and of your days in the tobacco plantation, I was beginning to think that the stories of your rakish behaviour might just be idle gossip," she said, "but I see now that you're every bit as forward as they say."

"And yet," he said, "we are dancing."

"I don't want my mother in a frenzy," she said.

"I do so love you," said the Earl. "Spirited — yet compassionate. Tempestuous — yet temperate."

The waltz was now accelerating, and the Earl seized Arabella in the hold known as *the imprisonment,* which was a waltz embrace decidedly *not* very genteel. "Your Lordship!" Arabella said in a whimper, but His Lordship was already leading her into the thickest part of the throng, where couples where whirling with abandon. Indeed, they had a near-collision with the Queen.

Her Majesty called out to Arabella above the fray, "Why, Monsieur is a most energetic dance partner, with *very* unusual movements! I haven't had so much fun since before my husband went mad!"

"My *Tante* is having a splendid time with your blue Frenchman," said the Earl. "She hasn't been out very much, you know, what with the King's condition … and her own."

"Your Lordship should not be so liberal in your protestations of love," Arabella said, "considering that this is only our third meeting … or is it our second?"

"I have known you all my life, my dear, in a spiritual sense; it is only physically that we have not met each other that often; but oh, I mean to remedy that!"

"I haven't time for a man who treats me as nothing but a potential conquest … neither a footman nor an earl. Why, I shouldn't put up with you if you were the Prince of Wales himself!"

"You seem to be putting up rather effectively right now, my dear," said the Earl.

"I don't want to make a scene," she said.

"My dear ... you *are* a scene," he said suavely.

Arabella did not know what to think about the Earl. On the one hand, she could not deny that he intrigued her. He was nothing like what she had expected, despite all the stories. His bravado was for show. Yet what was it hiding? Was there a human being in there somewhere, or was his façade simply a shell to conceal a total emptiness?

Was he the kind of wild animal that she could tame? And if she could not, what about the advantages she could enjoy as a Countess? Would she be forced to convert, and to suffer the symbols of popery in her very home? Would the Earl consider something as radical as a ... mixed marriage?

These were the thoughts that consumed her as she gave herself into the infectious rhythm of the waltz, and the ballroom swirled about her. Her world became a kaleidoscope. The intrigue, the bickering, the gossip seemed as naught.

Mrs. Dorrit, whose tête-à-tête with the Monsieur had been usurped by no less a figure than the Queen of England, had been relegated to a corner, where her brother had been sitting, grimly sipping a glass of wine.

"Catholics!" he muttered as she sat beside him.

"My dear brother," she said, "they really seem no different from us. I've seen no Satanic rites, or babies being sacrificed, all evening."

"One must read between the lines," he said, "peer behind the arras."

"I don't think a well-mannered person should be reading

between or peering *behind,*" said Mrs. Dorrit. "I've never peered behind *you,* my dear brother. What might I discover, I wonder?"

"I'm a man of God, through and through," he said. "Flawed, of course, but I trust that my occasional lapse does not interfere with my calling."

Mrs. Dorrit put down her glass and stared at Mr. Bumbry. How much had he had to drink? She had never known him to even remotely hint at any dark secret. Was he having an occasional dalliance with a milkmaid? Her brother seemed to realize that he might have said too much, and fell silent.

The Earl whirled past, positively flinging Arabella about his person, and she was shrieking with laughter.

"Catholics," said Mr. Bumbry again.

"We're not here to peer behind any arrases today, dear brother," said Mrs. Dorrit. "We are here to make notes about suitable matches for our girls."

"*Your* girls, my dear," said Mr. Bumbry.

In another corner of the ballroom, Lord Chuzzlewit was introducing Miss Anna to Signora Sforzando, who was actually mingling with the guests, none of whom seemed particularly shocked that an *actress* was wandering in their midst.

"Miss Anna is an accomplished pianist," said Lord Chuzzlewit. "And the Signora is our second queen, for she reigns supreme in Covent Garden as its most fragrant flower."

"Charmed," Miss Anna said, slightly nonplussed to be introduced to someone of the Signora's dubious social standing.

The diva threw her arms around Anna, discombobulating her further, and kissed her on both cheeks. "So delighted to meet a fellow artist!" she said. "His Lordship has told me of your overwhelming renditions of the nocturnes of Mr. Field."

"It is nothing, Signora," Anna said, "my mother always taught me to keep working on my accomplishments so I should be able to snare a husband from amongst all these louts."

"Heavens!" said His Lordship.

"I do love her plain speaking," said the Signora. "It's so refreshing to find it in the upper middle classes, who are so earnestly trying to ape what they think *actual* aristocrats should be like. Did they but know the truth!"

Another shock — the Signora plainly considered herself to be of a *higher* station than the Dorrits of this world. What a topsy-turvy world she must come from!

"My dear … you shall come up to the stage … you shall play, and I shall sing."

She made a grand gesture, and the orchestra halted in mid-phrase.

"Your Majesty, my Lords and Ladies, and … *others*," said the Signora in resonant, operatic tones, "Miss Anna Dorrit and I shall perform a duet."

There was enthusiastic applause. But when she looked up at the stage area, Anna started to panic. "There's no pianoforte," she said.

"Ah, but you are a great musician. Surely you can accompany me on something. There's a harp on the stage. I'm sure the harp must be one of your minor accomplishments ..."

Her Majesty spoke up. She was still with Monsieur Clatoux and they seemed to have been deep in conversation. "Nothing newfangled, *Schätzchen*," she said. "De King and We are old-fashioned; anything later than de music of Herr Handel sounds most horribly *avant-garde* to Us."

"*Cara mia*," said the Signora, "do you happen to know Mr. Handel's *V'adoro pupille*? That has a large harp part."

"Well ... I know the melody of course ... it is very famous ... yet ..." Despairingly, she glanced at Monsieur Clatoux. The alien merely gave her a wave of encouragement, as though to tell her it would be fine.

Never having touched a harp in her life — for, as the Signora pointed out, a member of the *upper middle classes* could hardly be expected to afford such an instrument in her home — Anna sat at the bench. The minute her hands touched the strings, she found herself bathed in an eerie blue light. Monsieur was about to work another miracle!

Her fingers worked of their own accord. She knew the music, of course, knew this air of Cleopatra from the opera *Giulio Cesare* very well ... and she had but to imagine the sounds in her head when her fingers began their nimble dance, and in a moment, the Signora began to warble with more delicacy and more virtuosity than any nightingale. The finely turned ornamentation, the sweetness of tone fueled Anna's passion and she played with an astonishing sensitivity of touch, her fingers reacting to every inflection her mind could conjure. Her feet seemed to intuit exactly where the pedal changes should come (luckily there were few in this archaic piece) and when they arrived, after a spine-tingling cadenza by the diva, at the da capo, Anna ornamented wildly, colouring every phrase with some curious melisma or inventive turn.

The applause was hearty and long, and, as she stepped down from the stage, Miss Anna was so overwhelmed she feared she would be unable to breathe. Indeed, she could feel a swoon coming on, despite not having laced her corset that tightly. She fell into the arms of her cousin, Lord Chuzzlewit, provoking a second round of applause.

Her Majesty waved for silence. "I haff not had dis much merriment in an age," she said.

The throng bowed and applauded.

"It is Our most royal pleasure," the Queen continued, "dis Dorrit family, along with Monsieur Clatoux, shall come to tea in Our own small cottage in Kew in a week's time."

Anna, still in a half swoon, glanced at her mother, who seemed about to faint herself. Only Arabella, of her family members, retained any kind of poise. She and the Earl were smiling as if it was they who had pulled off this coup.

It was quite late when the barouche arrived at the vicar's cottage. The help were still awake, though, and came to the door, all dying, it seemed, to hear the news.

Mrs. Dorrit sat for a while as her daughters and brother alighted. Receiving the favour of royalty, in the sight of the whole ton, had finally given her family a visible place in society. She watched contentedly as her daughters went inside, warmed by the awareness that, whatever went on at the ball, their lives as young women of Little Chiswick had truly begun.

Only Monsieur Clatoux remained outside.

The starlight lit up his soft, blue skin. His eyes twinkled, catching their cold light.

"At last," he said. "We are alone. Shall we go straight to your chamber?   Or shall we mate out here, in the orchard?"

17

Defenestrated and Deflowered

"Surely you jest," said Mrs. Dorrit, who perhaps secretly feared that the alien *was* speaking in jest. As the barouche waited for the rest of the party to leave Flanders House, she took the opportunity to say more. "Though, since I am a widow, I am in no danger of being ruined, nor would my marital prospects be particularly damaged by a ... dalliance ... though I'm sure I have no idea how one would actually ... I mean, the late Mr. Dorrit was fairly furtive in his fitful fumblings...."

"Heavens," said Monsieur Clatoux. "Do you always alliterate when you're aroused?"

"I think, thankfully, not," she said, suddenly realizing she had done it again.

It was too late for any further conversation, for the rest

of the family were piling into the barouche, and as it was but the second-best one on the estate, there was a great deal of squishing, squashing, and dovetailing of limbs; the latter entailed a most unseemly propinquity with Monsieur. Luckily it was dark enough that no one could notice how Mrs. Dorrit was blushing to the very gills.

Once they had arrived at the cottage, the girls were chattering about the adventures of the evening and could not wait to get to their room; meanwhile, Mr Bumbry, for some reason, decided to go and help Japheth with the horses; at the stoop, she found herself, unaccountably, alone once more with the blue-skinned Frenchman.

"I shall come to you in the night," said Monsieur Clatoux. "Once the others are asleep."

"Then I shall be asleep too," said Mrs. Dorrit. "You shall do nothing of the kind."

"I don't believe you shall be asleep at all," said the monsieur, "for I sense a certain ... palpitation in your pheromonal signature that suggests you may be in oestrus."

"Heavens! Oestrus?" said Mrs. Dorrit. She did not know what the word meant, but she was certain it was improper. "I am long past such *wicked* things!"

"Age cannot wither her," said the alien, "nor custom stale her infinite variety."

"If you think that flattery can restore that which I lost ... perhaps before I even found it...." Mrs. Dorrit murmured. The alien had a way of rendering her weak and confused, almost as though she were a young girl again. "I was

"Hardly flattery," said Monsieur. "I was but quoting your national poet, the Swan of Avon."

"I shall assuredly lock my door," said Mrs. Dorrit, "as I have always done since the late Mr. Dorrit passed away." So saying, she swept into the house and up the stairs, toward the relative isolation and reassuring clutter that was her room.

And yet, Mrs. Dorrit could not sleep. She twisted and tossed about, and when she closed her eyes, she imagined scenes from her marriage, scenes she had never dared revisit. Gruntings and gropings in the dark. Mr. Dorrit, fully clothed, of course, bearing down upon her as he attempted to unbutton his flies with the wrong hand, stroking her cheek with the other, rasping out endearments.

She had to admit it. *I bore him children,* she told herself ... *and yet I did not feel ... that heady fire of passion poets talk about.* She tried to conjure up a remembrance of such a feeling, but could not. *Perhaps I was not prepared to face the torrid torrent of desire,* she thought. *Perhaps I have buried such fragmentary notions so deep I cannot dig them up again.*

Yet, she reflected, she had lived a goodly life, and borne intelligent, if wayward girls, and they might even, against all odds, be on their way being well matched, climbing higher in the hierarchy of the ton that she ever dreamed possible.

She heard a tapping at the door.

I must resist! she told herself. *I am above all, respectable, of decent birth, and the sister of a clergyman!* She shrank back into the bed, almost as though Monsieur had already beaten down the door. But the tapping became no louder, and at length it seemed to stop.

Mrs. Dorrit tried to feel a measure of relief; instead, however, more memories — nay, rather, non-memories — of passion unfulfilled assailed her thoughts. But every image of her husband that sprang to mind became mixed with the sensation of Monsieur Clatoux, dovetailing against her calves on the barouche, each bump in the road sending both a chill and a wave of heat up and down her spine. What was it about the Monsieur? Was it a power only *foreign* men possessed?

She needed to concentrate her thoughts only on the late Mr. Dorrit. What had he looked like? Could she really not remember? Why was the heady aroma of Monsieur Clatoux filling her nostrils, rather than the earthy, pungent sweaty smell of Mr. Dorrit?

She got out of bed again, pulling her dressing-gown about her shoulders. She went to the window. She looked out over the woods, in the direction of the main house, knowing what lay beyond; the family plot, where the remains of dear Mr. Dorrit rested. Though he was probably turning over in his grave at this very moment, she reflected, considering the decidedly impure thoughts that were impinging on her consciousness.

As though to light up her dilemma, the full moon emerged from a cloud. The nightscape was transformed. The woods were silvered. The clouds seemed to scatter, giving a clear line of sight to the family's burial ground. She could see the memorial ... *too* clearly. It was unnatural. She felt as though she was floating. Suddenly, she realized that she *was*.

Mrs. Dorrit had somehow managed to sift through the panes like broth through a colander.

She had defenestrated herself and was wafting in the breeze. Or had she left her corporeal form behind? Was Mrs. Dorrit's body still in the bedroom, her nose still plastered to the window? The wind grew stronger. She could not look back, could not fight the force that was dragging her inexorably towards her late husband's grave.

And then she was standing here. The moon was dazzling. The gravestone shimmered with soft reflected light. Daffodils were everywhere, swaying in the breeze.

"Oh, Mr. Dorrit," she whispered — for during their years together she had never been so bold as to have addressed him by his Christian name — "how can you forgive me these terrible thoughts?"

Behind the headstone stood a tall marble cross, part of the more elaborate monument for the Lord Chuzzlewit, grandfather of the current possessor of the title, who had been somewhat unheroically done in by a misbehaving cannon during that embarrassing fracas in the American colonies. As Mrs. Dorrit gazed at her husband's grave, the cross seemed to grow in size and brilliance ... and she became aware that there was someone *on* the cross ... a shadowy Jesus, a silhouette against the powerful glow of the cross.

Mrs. Dorrit was a little nonplussed. Wasn't the image of a crucified Christ a vulgar display of papist idolatry? Unless she was experiencing a vision of the *actual* Jesus...

The apparition spoke softly. She trembled. The words were full of beauty and comfort. "My dear Mrs. Dorrit," it said. "Your husband has ascended to the angels. While you are on this beautiful earth, you must avail yourself of its pleasures. For the joys of Heaven are beyond your imagining. Yet in the joys of Earth, you can at least taste a shadow of their essence...."

"My Lord!" she whispered in rapture.

Then she noticed that the figure that she had thought to be a manifestation of God himself was naked ... and blue.

"Blasphemy!" she shrieked.

Too late! Monsieur Clatoux had descended from the cross and was even now enfolding her in his luxuriant embrace.

"How dare you! You clothe your craven lusts in the panoply of the church!"

She would have said more, but Monsieur stopped her mouth with a kiss that sent her entire body into a paroxysm of shuddering ecstasy. She had never known that the tongue could be used in such a way. And Monsieur's tongue was a chameleon, splitting into a dozen tendrils that simultaneously explored every corner of her mouth, stroking the inside of her cheeks, even flicking her vocal cords so that she thrummed with the unearthly music that came from them.

Pulling away, Monsieur whispered, "I've had every gender of my species ... except the female. You shall be the crowning glory of my erotic adventures!" He seemed to have twenty hands, as he unbuttoned stays, loosened corsets and teased seams with the skill of a master. She did not dare to look as one hand found something in her nether parts that no one had ever manipulated in such a way. She screamed with delight. And then she felt something else within her petticoats ... and she knew at once that Monsieur's engine of desire was capable of as much metamorphosis as his tongue, as it swelled into a precise and lubricious tightness.

"What is happening to me?" Mrs. Dorrit exclaimed.

"You are experiencing a second defloration, my dear Mrs. Dorrit. For, though you have previously experienced penetration, you have yet to drink from the wellsprings of your species' passion."

He lifted her in his arms and laid her down atop Lord Chuzzlewit's monument. She found herself moving to a music she had never known. The stone was softening. As she breached the heights, she realized that she was back in her own bed ... *What a relief!* she told herself. *This is a dream.*

And she yielded herself up completely, letting the ocean of pleasure wash over her.

But in the morning, she awoke to find her bed strewn with daffodils....

18

Appropriate Fashions

Miss Arabella Dorrit noticed, the morning after the ball, that her mother was not her usual self. At breakfast, she seemed to be walking on air. By mid-morning tea, she was sulking, at luncheon, pouting; at tea-time, again in the clouds; at dinner, her head was buried in the eel pie; at supper, she seemed bewildered. In short, she wore a different mood during each of the six customary meals of the day.

Her sister, meanwhile, took no meals at all; rather, she sat at the pianoforte, painstakingly taking on one étude after another.

Her uncle was rarely to be found; since the ball, he had been composing a very special — at least, so he deemed it — sermon, one that would come to Rubicon-like conclusions about the Earl's return to Flanders House. For some reason, composing this sermon entailed riding about on the estate and communing with God in the midst of nature, accompanied only by the manservant, Japheth.

Most absent of all was Monsieur Clatoux, who seemed to be spending all his time ensconced in his vehicle, not emerging for meals at all. Concerned with his health, and made restive by Anna's continual exertions on the pianoforte, Arabella ventured out into the garden, hoping that Monsieur Clatoux could provide some little diversion.

When she entered the spaceship, however, she found Monsieur attached to the wall by a series of straps, with various needles inserted into his orifices. His hands were losing shape, turning sometimes into lobster-like appendages or panther paws.

"Why, Monsieur!" she cried out. "Whatever is happening to you?"

Monsieur's lips moved, but what came out was a multilingual, meandering monologue: *"Electron tempesta zisixenxe los muertos chandrasekhar booby diolch yn fawr...."*

"Monsieur, I pray! One language at a time, that I might endeavour to comprehend your distress!"

Jagged sparks of purple lightning emanated from the straps holding Monsieur to the wall. The Frenchman screamed. *"Laissez-faire!"* he shrieked. *"La plume de ma tante! Rendezvous avec Rama! Le prince d'Aquitaine à la tour abolie!"*

At least he was down to a single language, thought Arabella. Now, to see if he can make sense. *"Qu'est que c'est votre problème?"* she ventured. Her French barely covered the weather and simple small talk, but perhaps whatever was ailing Monsieur could be explained within her limited vocabulary.

He continued in French for some time, making very little sense. At last, he sank into a kind of stupor.

"Monsieur!" Arabella said, running up to him and, disregarding all propriety, swabbing at his sweating brow with a fold of her sleeve.

He gasped. "Yesterday's exertions ... the splendour of the mating ... a magnificent woman, isn't she?"

"I'm sure I don't know what you mean. Who? Queen Charlotte?"

"My life force is depleting ... now ... I regenerate ... but cannot ... many more times...."

"Regenerate? For how long?" said Miss Arabella.

"At least ...one hundred ... of your hours...."

"Please, Monsieur. Regenerate as long as you wish. We have the visit to the Queen at Kew Palace in a week. You must at least survive until then! I am continuing to strive for the earliest opportunity to take you to the Mechanical Exhibition in London, so you can finally operate your telephonic device...."

"Leave me now!" Monsieur Clatoux moaned. "You must not see ... my true form!"

He began to shake. The wall rattled. Tentacles began issuing from him, bursting open his chemise. Blue, gooey fluids began spurting. Arabella was terrified. She could not help staring —

"Go!" said Monsieur. "Before you too ... undergo meta ... mor .. phosis!"

Monsieur did not emerge for days, but much needed to be done. Most importantly, there were the clothes to consider. "This is not a ball," said Mrs. Dorrit to her children, "so flamboyance for its own sake is by no means *de rigueur.* Rather, a combination of elegance and humility is required. But we must not by any stretch of the imagination appear to be members of the ..." she shuddered ..."middle classes."

"Why, mother dear," Arabella said sweetly, "but surely we are."

"Your second cousin is a Baron!" her mother said reprovingly.

"And our uncle is a parson," Arabella retorted.

"Not *another* dress!" Anna said.

Arabella pointed out that, in his debilitated state, Monsieur would probably not be able to manufacture enough golden guineas for any more couture. "We should not tax him so," she said. "Why, he is still recovering from the aftermath of the ball!"

She wondered why her mother looked at her so after that remark. She actually seemed to be concealing some dark secret; which was notable because her mother had no secrets, dark or otherwise.

"Mother dear, pray do not be so upset; I do not think it was you who caused Monsieur's malaise." At which her mother looked at the floor. Arabella was even more convinced that something *very* peculiar was going on.

Indeed, as the days went by, and Monsieur did not emerge from his vehicle, it became evident that no new wardrobe would be forthcoming, and Arabella had to help her mother improvise something serviceable out of what they had. Mrs. Dorrit did have things in chests she had not worn in an age. With the help of the scullery maid and the housekeeper, and a few spare satin curtains, they were able to create a credible imitation of the work of the ladies Pirandello *and* Beaumarchais!

"You may look a little bizarre," said Mrs. Dorrit, "but we do have the advantage; Monsieur is French, and thus, by definition, he has introduced us to the latest Paris fashions, as yet unseen in Little Chiswick."

"But this bonnet you've created, Mama," said Miss Arabella. "I daresay I shall frighten the peacocks." For it was well known that Queen Charlotte kept a veritable zoo at Kew. Indeed, it was a formidable spectacle, with feathers from all manner of fowl, plucked from discarded hats and reassembled atop a turban fashioned from a tablecloth.

"You are no designer, mama," said Miss Anna, "but you certainly have a flair for the eccentric."

"I do comprehend," said Mrs. Dorrit, "appropriate fashions."

It took the entire week for the three intrepid women to design their wardrobe *manqué*, but when it was done, even Mr. Bumbry was impressed. Indeed, he quoted St. Matthew's gospel: "Heavens! even Solomon in all his glory was not arrayed like one of these."

"Perhaps so," said Mrs. Dorrit, "but I can assure you, my dear brother, that a lot more toiling and spinning went into these costumes than we can discern in the sixth chapter of Matthew."

But it was not until the morning of the Dorrits's departure for Kew Palace that Monsieur Clatoux emerged from his "regeneration process." They ladies were already in front of the cottage, waiting for the barouche to arrive from the manor — for it would not do to visit royalty in the second-best.

The spaceship opened up and Monsieur Clatoux stepped forth, at which point Mrs. Dorrit let forth a piercing squeal of surprise and delight. *What could have got into Mama?* Arabella thought. And then she saw....

The creature that emerged from the bowels of the starship was so dazzling, Mrs. Dorrit was practically blinded. For the man she beheld was clothed not in silks, but in the very fabric of rainbow, that somehow had been woven into a cutaway coat. His pantaloons had whirling red stripes like twin barber's poles. A cloak, seeming to flap about of its own accord though there was no wind, had a phosphorescent glow. He sported an amazing hat that seemed to be an extension of his own hair. Around his head, a soft halo glowed.

Mrs. Dorrit was gasping. Her daughters were laughing. Mr. Bumbry, who had arrived in the barouche with Japheth, sat agape.

"Is it too much?" said Monsieur Clatoux.

"Ah ... perhaps so," Mrs. Dorrit managed to say.

"I see. I shall tone it down a little. Not the halo, at any rate. One shouldn't want to out-queen the queen."

19

Kangaroo Court

Although Monsieur Clatoux did tone down his appearance somewhat, so that he no longer looked like Elijah ascending in his chariot, he was still splendid. Only Miss Arabella knew what he had gone through to render himself once more palatable to the regard of humans. Solicitously, she approached him as they started to board the barouche.

"Do not concern yourself, my dear," said Monsieur. "I know how important this royal tea is to your family's standing in the ton. You have been good to me, and it is my duty, nay, my supreme pleasure to aid you all in achieving your goals."

"But ... that process by which you ... restored

yourself..."

"That is true. It is the last time. The amount of *effluvium vitae* that remains would barely be enough to sustain me at full capacity for a day or two; yet, we shall cross that bridge when we get there, shall we not? I am a viable being for the time being, and if I succeed in communicating with my *zngenxip*, all will be well."

Arabella had no idea what a *zngenxip* might be, but it certainly sounded portentous. "If you need a *zngenxip* to be well, Monsieur, I shall do my utmost to bring you into contact with one! But do turn off that halo, Monsieur, or Her Majesty will go blind!"

To be fair, it was barely two miles from Little Chiswick to Kew Palace, so it was hardly the wanderings of Ulysses. Yet, for Arabella, it was an odyssey rarely undertaken. The ladies in their repurposed plumage, the "toned-down" but still ostentatious Frenchman, and the sober clergyman made altogether a spectacle as they moved, with measured slowness, through the main street. "Slower, Japheth, I pray!" Mrs. Dorrit kept saying. We want everyone in the *ton* to know that today we take tea with the Queen of England herself!"

Thus they continued their progress, crossing the bridge where couples and chaperones could be observed promenading in their best attire, and past a few more shops and finally into open country; uninhabited save for the odd cow grazing far from the herd. "What bliss!" Mrs. Dorrit exclaimed. "To be travelling! To discover alien shores and strange lands!"

"We are but half a mile from home, sister," Mr. Bumbry

said gruffly.

"And how often have I been even this far?" said Mrs. Dorrit.

"You did go to your cousin's two years ago," said Mr. Bumbry. "That was twenty miles at the least."

"That was quite an adventure," Mrs. Dorrit said.

Kew, too, was an adventure. As soon as the barouche passed the front gate, Mrs. Dorrit knew she was breathing the rarefied air of a royal presence. They had been invited to the "cottage" — as Her Majesty called it — it was a cottage in the sense that their own residence was a dog kennel. As they approached, a dozen footmen approached, splendidly bewigged and in immaculate livery.

An even more resplendent steward appeared to lead them to the Queen, dressed as though he had stepped out of a hundred-year-old painting. The party was conducted through halls and staterooms, but Mrs. Dorrit saw no sign of a tea-service anywhere. Until they passed through a rear entrance and found themselves in a garden. A creature leapt out of the bushes.

"Heavens!" said Mrs. Dorrit. The animal jumped out of the way, slapping its tail on the grass.

"Ah!" came the familiar, teutonic voice. "Dat is one of Our kangaroos. She is called Gudrun. Exotic, is she not?"

The most extraordinary thing happened then. Monsieur Clatoux began to utter a series of grunting, barking noises. Gudrun was spellbound, and immediately leapt into Monsieur's arms, moving in a manner that seemed suspiciously unseemly … a bacchanalian variant of a waltz.

"*Mein Gott!* She loves you, my strange Frenchman!" said

the Queen. "But, please, I pray you, sit and enjoy dis weather."

Remembering her manners in time, Mrs. Dorrit curtsied and motioned for her daughters to do the same. "Your Majesty," she murmured.

But Her Majesty seemed interested only in the Frenchman. "You know Paris, denn, We take it?"

"Like the back of my hand," said Monsieur.

"Ah! You shall guide Us!" she said. "But, We hope, not in dis silly costume. We prefer to see you as We did at de ball."

"But I created these garments precisely for your delectation, Your Majesty. Of course, I shall be happy to remove them if you should give me occasion."

"Ha! It is to laugh!" said the Queen. "We are married. We are a Queen. You must ... *Respekt haben.* But Paris..."

"We can go now if you like, Your Majesty," he said. "I have but to summon my ship." He managed to extricate himself from the kangaroo's embrace, only to be assaulted by a marmoset.

"No, no, little one!" he said, and then proceeded to make a series of trills, twitters, and tooting noises. The marmoset seemed crestfallen, and slunk off into the bushes.

"A veritable St. Francis!" said a familiar voice.

"Mon cher cousin!" said the Queen. *"So eine Überraschung!* Such a surprise!"

To Mrs. Dorrit's amazement, the Earl was walking down the pathway from the cottage, whistling. "Why, he speaks the language of every animal, does he not?" He looked at Arabella. "Why, did you not know I was coming? Tante Charlotte sent me a note; I would have sent you a *billet-*

doux, but I hardly had time to mount my steed and race to your side."

"*Mon cousin*, you must show Arabella de menagerie."

The Earl put forth his arm, and he and Arabella were off before Mrs. Dorrit could remark upon the lack of a chaperone.   Though, this being the royal palace, she could not very well object to the command of a Queen.

From deeper into the garden, *another* man emerged ... Lord Chuzzlewit! So this was not to be a little tête-à-tête, but a full-blown garden party!   Mrs. Dorrit wondered when the croquet sticks would appear.

"No croquet, my dear," said the Queen, seeming to read her mind. "It confuses de kangaroos."

And indeed, more kangaroos were popping in.

"Anna!" Lord Chuzzlewit said, as if surprised. "You are a sight today!   I have never seen anything quite so ... colourful."

"We just cut up the bloody curtains," Anna said.   The Queen giggled. "You naughty Parisians!" she said, wagging a finger at Monsieur.

Unfazed, Lord Chuzzlewit continued, "Pray, come for a perambulation about this beautiful garden.   There is a pagoda you simply must see, built in the style of Chinamen, and adorned with dozens of dragons." He took Miss Anna by the arm, and they left abruptly.

More kangaroos were emerging now, and all seemed enamoured of the Frenchman. They encircled him, hopping about and barking in a kind of marsupial ecstasy.

It appeared that Mrs. Dorrit was the only member of her family not otherwise engaged, for her daughters had gone off and Mr. Bumbry was wandering about, peering at the

peacocks. The marmoset, meanwhile, was the only creature actually drinking tea, which it did daintily, holding
the handle between two of its digits while stirring with its
tail. Mrs. Dorrit felt a little discomfited, especially when
the Queen began to ask questions of a rather intimate nature.

"Dis Frenchman," said Her Majesty. "His prowess at de
art of love … *gut, ja?*"

"Your Majesty!" said Mrs. Dorrit, before she remembered
that those in the uppermost ranks of society do not have to
follow the rules of normal folk, and that the King, though
he be mad as a hatter, possessed the *divine right of kings,*
and thus he, and his, need not obey the strictures of con-
ventional morality.

"Come," said the Queen. "We may speak, for he is … at
de moment … engaged mit de kangaroos. We, too, have
seen him, how you say, naked. *Wie groß!*"

"Indeed, Your Majesty," said Mrs. Dorrit, absently
adding more sugar to her tea than she quite intended, and
quite forgetting to butter her scone.

"Let Us take anodder look!" said the Queen. "Monsieur!
Monsieur!"

But the Frenchman was nowhere to be seen, and the
kangaroos were chattering and hopping in a frenzy.

"He has a habit of disappearing," said Mrs. Dorrit. "But
then, he reappears with equal alacrity."

"We want de Frenchman!" said Her Majesty. "And not
de kangaroos!" She looked at Mrs. Dorrit with what appeared to be something of a conspiratorial look. "Are we
not old women, *du und ich?*" she said. "Shall we not feast
our eyes before we die?"

"Well, since you put it that way, Your Majesty," said Mrs. Dorrit, who assuredly had not forgotten the heights of passion she had scaled just the week before, when the Frenchman's infinitely malleable, not to mention inflatable, engine of desire had filled her to the very brim.

At that moment, a strange high-pitched whine pierced the air. It segued into a kind of whistling, with a sort of trill in the middle. Then came another sound, sweeter than the first. And another. Birdsong … but what melodious birdsong! One song, two songs, weaving about each other in a duo of delight.

"Donnerwetter! St. Francis has found his equal!" said the Queen. "Quick! before he is making de kangaroos go mad!"

Following the sounds, Mrs. Dorrit went down a pathway, then another. At length she reached a clearing. There were birds everywhere … real birds and mechanical ones … and gilded cages set on various plinths and hanging from branches. The birds were all singing … and quite a cacophony it was … but above that sound was the sound of Monsieur Clatoux, who was chirping up a storm. And not to be outdone was a raggedy plump fellow in a soiled nightshirt, from whose lips issued a melodious counterpoint.

The Dorrits's Frenchman was duelling birdsong with Mad King George himself! And His Majesty was flapping his arms and daintily hopping about, as though he were himself one of the caged birds that surrounded him!

"Horrors!" said the Queen. "Well, at least he is not mourning his lost America."

"America?" the King roared. "I heard that! Oh, America, America!" And he began to weep.

"I should not have reminded him!" said Her Majesty.

"Nein," said the King, "you should not, my dear, sweet Charlotte. Oh, oh, America!" The clearing became crowded now as marmosets and kangaroos began arriving, ensorcelled by the beauty of the Frenchman's song, and mindful of the King's profound melancholy.

Monsieur's singing became even more delicate now. He sounded like a nightingale. At this, the King seemed a little less sad. Yet in a few moments came another fit of weeping.

"If only I could … please cheer him up," said the Queen. "Always he is dis way, weeping for America."

"But Your Majesty," said the Frenchman at last. "What if I could show you another America? An America you did not lose, a shiny new America that you will never lose? Would that not make you happy?"

"You can do dat?" said the Queen. "He would be cured! It would be magic!"

"When sufficiently advanced," said Monsieur Clatoux, "any technology is indistinguishable from magic."

20

Another Country

And indeed, what happened next did appear to be magic.

His Majesty, still weeping over lost America, was ensconced in a kind of throne-cum-sedan-chair that attendants had brought over from the house. At His Majesty's right hand, Monsieur stood, waving his arms about like a cerulean-skinned Prospero.

Behind the King, Queen Charlotte had crept up and was also gazing at the unfolding spectacle.

And as events proceeded, Mrs. Dorrit could see that her daughters, each accompanied by — dared she ever hope — the ton's most desirable of beaux — also stood in the bushes. The only one nowhere to be seen was Mr. Bumbry. Perhaps he was off trying to teach religion to the benighted Japheth.

What unfolded before Mrs Dorrit's eyes was this:

First, it seemed that the sky was splitting down the middle, and it was actually the two halves of a massive blue theatrical curtain. The piece of land they were on, a little square of the garden behind Queen Charlotte's cottage, seemed to detach itself from the ground and turn into a kind of grassy flying carpet. This, as it were, carpet rose into the air, leaving behind an exact copy of itself.

Indeed, Mrs. Dorrit, looking back down to terra firma, saw Their Majesties, herself, her daughters and their prospects all standing there, their features all frozen in a kind of idiotic stare, their mouths all agape.

As their verdant platform gathered speed, Mrs. Dorrit saw them burst through the curtain of sky which parted to receive them. Presently they were above the ocean. She could hear the whistling of the wind, but she could feel no wind, though they were flying faster than any horse-drawn carriage.

"Heavens!" she said. "We must be going at more than twenty miles an hour!"

As they smashed through a low cloud, Monsieur said, "Three thousand miles an hour, to be precise."

"But why haven't we been blown off this rather, ah, precarious perch?" Mrs. Dorrit said.

"We are encased in a forcebubble with a nano-gyro-stabilizers. The sound of the wind is synthesized to give a more congenial atmosphere than the hermetically sealed bubble, which cannot admit any external sound at all, can sustain."

"Good Heavens!" said the King. "Nano-gyro, eh! And the sound effects for relaxation — an exquisite touch!"

It seemed to Mrs. Dorrit that His Majesty was spouting the same nonsense that Monsieur was. Or was it nonsense? For they continued in the same vein for quite some moments, and she started to wonder whether it was not nonsense, after all, not the kind of hocus-pocus that a conjurer declaims to hide his own sleight of hand.

Could it be that King George was not insane at all, but actually some kind of genius?

Surely not! That would undermine the very basis of Mrs. Dorrit's reality!

But His Majesty and the Frenchman continued their conversation without even, it seemed, coming up for air. They spoke of mu-mesons, of quantum entanglement, and of special relativity ... or was it special relations? His Majesty even laughed! And then the two of them began exchanging birdcalls, and discussing mating rituals of the greater and lesser tits. Were she able to understand their conversation, she did not doubt but that the subject matter was a little off-colour. Thank goodness, she did not have all the education that comes to a man!

Turning to look at her daughter Arabella, she was somewhat appalled to see that she was observing the dialogue with rapt attention, doing her best, poor thing, to follow. Just like those scientific papers she loved so much ... no doubt imagining for herself some kind of meaning into those big words.

Presently, they espied land in the distance, and the flying piece of lawn began to descend toward earth. At length, they alighted on a what seemed to be a rooftop overlooking a city square. At its centre stood an impressive bronze statue of no less a personage than His Majesty himself.

The square was filling with people. Though there was no sound, one could see the crowd cheering. A line of redcoats was marching into the square, preceded by fifes and drums. The crowd was strewing flowers.

"This is a version of history where America was not lost," said Monsieur Clatoux, "and it is as real as the reality in which it was."

"Show me more," said the King.

As the party watched, the crowd began to move rapidly. "I am accelerating the time continuum viewscape," said Monsieur Clatoux. "Behold! A year in a second!" And now the entire spectacle became a blur and it seemed that whole buildings were forming and unforming. The buildings were growing, too, crawling upward to the sky.

"Why," said Mrs. Dorrit, "that tower over there must be twenty storeys high!"

"A hundred, actually," said the Frenchman, as the tower blotted out the sun. "We have reached the twentieth century. Come, I shall slow things down."

What an unmitigated spectacle! Mrs. Dorrit gazed at a scene she could not have imagined. The people were attired outlandishly — some, it seemed, only in undershirts, and all the ladies were vastly plump, and had not the decency to wear a decent corset. They filled the streets. More amazingly, the square was filled with an array of horseless carriages, which flowed back and forth in a kind of parade, sometimes stopping, sometimes turning down a side street, moving in lines unnaturally straight.

As Monsieur sped up time again, she saw some vehicles take flight, and actually fly *above* the streets, and these buildings — the Frenchmen called them *skyscrapers* —

climbed even higher, until no sunlight remained at all. Yet the area glowed from some artificial radiance.

"It is the twenty-first century," said the Frenchman. "The United States of Georgia cover half the world. Beyond the orbit of Saturn, there is a planet named George, and beyond, another named Charlotte, and beyond that still, a planetary cluster known as the Georgettes."

Mrs. Dorrit saw Arabella pay great attention to these absurd astronomical fantasies. Anna was distracted, chatting with Lord Chuzzlewit about the music of John Field.

"More!" said His Majesty.

"Your nerves, *mein Schatz!*" said the Queen. "You will have *ein* hysteria!"

Nothing loath, the Frenchman summoned up more visions beyond imagining. The Georgians of the future conquered first the moon, then Mars. Intrepid Georgians landed on a moon of George, then used it as a base from which to launch an exploration of the nearby stars ... and all was George, George, George, whatever direction one looked. The King cheered and sipped his tea.

Presently, exhausted from the barrage of impossible images, His Majesty dozed off, and Monsieur Clatoux reversed course, making time go backwards and sending them reeling back across the ocean — of time as well as space — to settle softly on the grass of Kew Palace, and to merge with the statue-like simulacra that had stood there, motionless, waiting to be refilled with consciousness.

At length, the King said, "You can see, my faithful subjects, that I not nearly as mad as you thought."

"Nay, rather," said Monsieur Clatoux, "His Majesty has merely crossed paths with another version of himself from another dimension, and has become depressed because he cannot return, and because those in this world can barely understand him."

"Summon Parliament!" said the King. "I shall dissolve it immediately, and rule by decree!"

"Dere, dere, *Schätzchen,*" said the Queen. "Better to be a madman denn a tyrant!"

"There has been enough interruption in this timeline, alas," said Monsieur. "A further anomaly could well result in the destruction of the entire universe."

"Well, We can't have that, what!" said the King.

"I think it's best to leave things as they are, Your Majesty," said Monsieur.

"Nevertheless, my magical Frenchman," said the King, "you have given Us a startling yet welcome vision of what might have been. We shall inhabit this world with far greater comfort, knowing that there is, in the infinite reaches, an Empire of Georgia."

"Thank you, Your Majesty."

"Well, normally We would give you half Our kingdom, or some other such trifle. We can't very well ennoble you — what would people think? — but I think —" He summoned his steward, who presently returned with a massive sword.

"You're not going to decapitate me, Your Majesty?"

"Heavens, no! We shall knight you! And, after tea, as we seem to have a quorum, We shall celebrate with a round of croquet!"

21

Tragic Mushrooms

Mrs. Dorrit was, not to put too fine a point on it, feeling on top of the world. Having bathed in the radiance of His Mad Majesty and Her Majesty the Queen, having actually bested the King at croquet — that alone would have been the high point of many a lifetime for a gentlewoman from Little Chiswick. But in addition, having her very own Frenchman knighted, her daughters on the verge of being spoken for, and herself having undergone the heady ecstasy of … well! … but she dared not actually give a name to the intimate union she had experienced.

Indeed, on their return from Kew, their lives seemed miraculously transformed. For every tea-time was now occupied by visitors, when once, no one would have given the Dorrits the time of day.

But now, each day brought suitors, gossips, and even music lovers desirous of hearing Anna perform the latest quadrilles on the pianoforte.

Today it was the grotesque Mrs. Sanditon who had come to tea, offering a basket of mushrooms she had gathered in the woods. Mrs. O'Keefe had swept them up with glee, and announced that she would make a mushroom catsup with bay leaves and vinegar, and use it to dress a haunch of venison that she had a-drying in the larder.

"We shall have a splendid feast of it," said Mrs. Dorrit.

"Since Mr. Sanditon perished from the consumption, I've had few feasts, splendid or otherwise," said Mrs. Sanditon, although her immense girth would tend to suggest otherwise.

"My brother, Mr Bumbry, is at church, preparing a sermon about the depravities of contemporary society," said Mrs. Dorrit, "and Monsieur has been feeling under the weather; he has not emerged from his hiding place for days. My Anna has been tending to him."

"And Miss Arabella?"

"She has gone over to the big house to, as she claims, read up on some scientific treatises from the Royal Society; and she has taken our maid-of-all-work along to keep an eye out for any knights errant. We are just two middle-aged gossips here, alas!" said Mrs. Dorrit. She wondered whether Mrs. Sanditon even *had* any gossip to share; certainly none could be as juicy as all that had transpired at Kew, but those events probably constituted a State Secret.

In spite of her doubts, Mrs. Sanditon soon began spewing forth scandal with alacrity. "Those Farthingale brothers! When they were spied spiriting off the two eldest Gotham-Clarkes, Edwina and Edna, to a questionable tête-à-tête in a graveyard, they each claimed to be chaperoning the other!"

"Fascinating!" Mrs. Dorrit *had* heard that one — from the maid-of-all-work, for Heaven's sake! — but was determined to appear agreeable, lest this woman speak ill of her at her next port of call. Grimly, she poured Mrs. Sanditon more tea. There was no need to inform her that she was imbibing from the second-best china.

"You must think my gossip awfully stale, what," said Mrs. Sanditon. "But let me speak of the *billet-doux* that the Gotham-Clarkes's scullery-maid unearthed!"

"Yes, why not?" said Mrs. Dorrit, snapping at her cucumber sandwich, and wishing that her daughters would come to alleviate the ennui.

Mrs. Sanditon began to expound in greatest detail on the contents of this putative epistle.

"My word!" said Mrs. Dorrit. "How came such a well-guarded letter into your possession?"

"Possession?" said Mrs. Sanditon, chuckling. "It is all but rumour."

"And rumour is but air," Mrs. Dorrit said, nodding sagely and pouring another cup. "I wonder how Mrs. O'Keefe is doing with the mushroom catsup?"

"There is a rumour," Mrs. Sanditon said, "of a newfangled recipe for catsup using tomatoes from America. Horrific, I'd say, and I'd never do anything to support those ungrateful miscreants."

"My daughter Arabella, who has pretensions to scientific

inquiry, has informed me that tomatoes are close relatives of the belladonna, and prone to be poisonous," Mrs. Dorrit said.

"Mushrooms are much safer," Mrs. Sanditon said.

At that moment, a piercing scream could be heard from the kitchen, followed by a crash. The screaming continued. Whatever could be wrong?

"Pandemonium in the pantry, my dear?" said Mrs. Sanditon. "Surely your butler —" She pretended to have forgotten, then started to tsk-tsking at her host's apparent paucity of household staff.

"Oh, dear," said Mrs. Dorrit. "I'd better find out if the poor dear has injured herself."

She rushed into the kitchen, leaving Mrs. Sanditon unattended. Mrs. O'Keefe was writhing about on the floor, foaming at the mouth.

"And Mrs. Sanditon was just saying *tomatoes* are poisonous," Mrs. Dorrit said, fuming. "How dare she!"

"I just ... was tasting the catsup ..." the housekeeper gasped. "Dear Lord, I think I'm dying!"

"A doctor?" said Mrs. Dorrit. "Perhaps Monsieur Clatoux can work a miracle ..."

She decided, whether Monsieur willed it or no, she must get him to intervene. As she returned to the tea-table, she saw that Mrs. Sanditon had not wasted a moment of her accidental privacy, and was already snooping in a drawer, doubtless hoping to find a few more stashed billets-doux for her collection of second-hand scandal.

"Explore all you wish," Mrs. Dorrit said. "You'll find no mysteries in *this* house. Now, I pray you, watch the housekeeper, for I must summon help."

"Watch a dying woman?" said Mrs. Sanditon. "Why, I never!"

"One whom *you* may have poisoned!" said Mrs. Dorrit, stalking out of the house, rushing across the garden, and banging on the wall of Monsieur Clatoux's spaceship.

"Come quickly!" she said as he emerged, wearing only his blue-skinned human form. "Mrs. O'Keefe has been struck by some deathly malady!"

"Let me synthesize some clothes," he said.

"No time for that," said Mrs. Dorrit. "I don't care if Mrs. Sanditon lays eyes on that … monstrous appendage of yours. Let her have something *real* to reveal at the next soirée!"

Monsieur Clatoux followed Mrs. Dorrit into the drawing-room and through to the kitchen, where her unwelcome guest was kneeling beside the shaking housekeeper. At the sight of Monsieur's fleshy protuberance, Mrs. Sanditon screamed, even more loudly than Mrs. O'Keefe.

"Which one is at death's door?" said Monsieur. "The merely fat one — or the *blancmange?*"

"Do not ridicule my condition, sir!" said Mrs. Sanditon. "I can't help overeating since my late husband —"

"If you don't wish to be ridiculed," said Monsieur, "you shouldn't expose yourself."

"Expose! And what, pray, is *that?*" said Mrs. Sanditon, pointing at the prodigious engine that had provoked her shrieks in the first place.

"Mother o' God," gasped Mrs. O'Keefe. "Who's the bloody patient here?" Not that this was not obvious, for the housekeeper had swollen to almost double her girth, and had turned a most unnatural shade of purple.

Monsieur pushed Mrs. Sanditon out the way. "Witty to the last," he said. He placed his ear to her chest. His demeanour became grave. "Mrs. Dorrit," he said, "I'm afraid that Mrs. O'Keefe's corporeal construct is malfunctioning."

"Whatever do you mean?" said Mrs. Dorrit, though she already divined the worst.

"She has indeed, been poisoned. And while I can synthesize a partial antidote, I shall need Mrs. O'Keefe's cooperation."

"But she is on death's door," said Mrs. Dorrit.

"My reagent can work," he said, "but whilst it is infusing into her bloodstream, it needs a catalyst, one produced naturally in the female body, a substance known to our science as *estrogen.*"

"What species of gobbledygook is this?"

"It's a hormone produced by women who are … in the throes of passion," said Monsieur.

"Heavens!" said Mrs. Dorrit. "Mrs. O'Keefe is a good woman, an upright woman. Do you want to say that, in order to restore her to life, she must —"

"It is an convenient coincidence," said Monsieur Clatoux, "that I have arrived without the encumbrance of clothing."

"No, no! I can't die in *sin*," Mrs. O'Keefe wailed. "I beg you, Mrs. Dorrit, get me a priest…."

"You mean summon Mr. Bumbry?"

"I do not!" said Mrs. O'Keefe, thrashing about. "I'm telling you, I need me last rites. I beseech you, mistress, a priest!"

"You mean a *Roman Catholic* priest?" She had no idea where one could find such a person … unless she ventured over to Flanders House unescorted. She gazed down at the woman who had faithfully served her household through thick and thin, still squirming and heaving.

"Mrs. Sanditon," Monsieur said with some urgency, "lift Mrs. O'Keefe's petticoats while I try to raise her hormone level." He transformed one finger into a kind of needle, and stabbed it into the supine woman's arm. As Mrs. Sanditon exposed the housekeeper's unmentionable region, Monsieur's diabolical device swelled to such a height that even Mrs. Dorrit, whose body had once entertained this selfsame organ within it, could barely suppress a squeal of shock and awe.

Mrs. Dorrit could not bear to look. Conflicting emotions warred within her as she thought of the agony Mrs. O'Keefe must be undergoing, yet knew the ecstasy Monsieur was capable of delivering. Surely, Monsieur's organ was even larger than she remembered. Would he rive her in twain whilst endeavouring to save her life?

"Lend me your driver!" she demanded of Mrs. Sanditon. "I shan't have Mrs. O'Keefe die without the comfort of her deluded faith. She shall have her popish pablum ere she perish."

So saying, she stormed from the kitchen and out into the garden, calling for Mrs. Sanditon's coach.

It was only when she was halfway to the Catholics' den of iniquity that it occurred to her to wonder why Anna had not emerged from the the Frenchman's vehicle, and whether Monsieur had been entertaining her daughter in the selfsame state of déshabillé.

22

Stuck in a Starship

Miss Anna had indeed been tending to Monsieur ... or, perhaps, as he should now be known, simply "Sir" Clatoux, if Clatoux was indeed his first name. He lay on a low couch inside his spaceship, and Anna was swabbing his forehead with a sponge, and he was moaning and shaking.

"Are there no salves or medicines you could create by transmutation?" Anna said.

"Alas, no; such remedies would work well on your species, but, created as they are from my own substance, my body would recognize their chemical structure as virtual rather than real, and they would not be efficacious. Nay, only a period of regeneration can help me, and the ship has barely enough power left for that ... I must conserve ... every possible erg of energy ..."

"But what can I do?" Anna said, despairing. "Perhaps a cup of tea?"

But Monsieur directed Anna to help him off the couch,

and to support him as he groped his way towards one of the ship's metallic walls. She half-dragged, half-pushed him as he backed into the wall. To Anna's distress, Monsieur's garments were dissolving and seemingly getting absorbed into his bare skin. Monsieur's characteristic fragrance spewed forth and filled her nostrils, awakening inchoate longings. "Monsieur!" she cried. "You are losing your clothes!"

"I must recycle the simulacra," he said. "I need every speck of spacetime back under my control."

Anna backed away, fearing an inadvertent arousal from her propinquity to Monsieur's rampant flesh. But the quarters were cramped, and the smell of the Frenchman was maddening. Monsieur seemed unaware of her discomfiture.

Monsieur began shaking as though palsied for a few moments. Then he seemed to pass out; his eyes rolled up in their sockets. Miss Anna said, "Monsieur, I really should leave; this is a little compromising … I'd be damned if I care, but my mother will be furious."

At that moment, there was a banging outside the ship and she could hear Mrs. Dorrit shrieking: "Mrs. O'Keefe! Our housekeeper! She is poisoned! Come quickly!"

Panicking, Anna shook Monsieur by the shoulders. He seemed as though dead. What should she do? What exactly was happening to the Frenchman? Despairing of being able to awaken him, she abandoned all caution, and kissed him passionately and firmly on the mouth.

Monsieur's lips quivered, then he jerked into consciousness. The rapping outside was more insistent now. Without a word, as though energised by Miss Anna's osculatory endeavours, he leapt up and made straight for the far wall. Still entirely naked, he passed through the metal as though it were thin air. The wall reconstituted itself in an instant and was seeamless.

When Anna tried to follow him out, the wall was utterly solid. The knocked, she banged with her fists.

Where was the puckering portal she remembered from when she entered? Or was the entrance just another of those illusions the spaceship could conjure up at will?

She realized that the spaceship had no actual door — not one that could be found in a single place, like normal doors with frames and handles. There would always been an opening whenever Monsieur needed there to be one. And there was *no* opening, if Monsieur Clatoux did not will one into existence.

"What am I to do?" she said.

It was just like in that tale from the *Arabian Nights,* the one with the cave and the forty thieves and *"Open sesame."*

Anna was trapped inside the alien vehicle, and Sir Clatoux had rushed out into the garden without his clothes; only the telltale scent remained. She was still tingling all over from it.

There had to be a way to leave the vehicle. Anna traversed the small chamber and found a passageway she was sure she had not seen before. She could barely squeeze through and she found herself in a kind of miniature arboretum, with purple plants and crablike bushes. The plants slithered about; they were not entirely rooted to the floor. There was something a bit tentacular about the vines, and the plants made a hissing sound as they moved. Anna tried to go back to the antechamber, but the passageway was no longer to be found.

Among the vegetation, there were some metallic protuberances, knobs and buttons. When Anna brushed against one of them, there was a whir. There were coloured lights, blinking on and off. Perhaps one of these buttons could open the spaceship so she could find out what the emergency was with Mrs. O'Keefe.

She tried a few more. The entire vehicle began shaking. Some of the plants detached themselves and were flying around above her head. Unearthly music filled the air, and she was seized with an urge to dance and sing. She pushed a few more buttons.

There was movement now. The entire spaceship was shaking and rattling as though it was readying itself to lift itself into the air — and then — she could feel the dizzying sensation of it in her head — the ship took off! But how? Where?

"No!" she cried out. "Not this! This isn't where I'm trying to go!"

Then where?

The voice filled her mind like a cup of sweet, milky tea, filling her with a sense of peace even though she was being thrown about the cabin and assaulted by sentient plants.

"Who are you?" she whispered. As she glanced around the chamber she realized the plants were all wiggling in time with the words. Somehow, the voice was coming from them and resonating inside her skull.

I am the ship itself, the voice said. I am the navigator. The comforter. An artificial mind created from a million memories. You have accessed me, but you are not my usual pilot. You are not even of the same species. Yet you have activated me and I am here to serve you.

"Take me back," said Miss Anna. "Back, I say!"

Of course. If you visualize your destination, we shall be there almost at once, for time and space are one.

Miss Anna closed her eyes. She tried to think of the garden. The quiet of the apple grove. Her mother, waiting at the door. But the images would not come. Instead, a passionate music was raging like a tempest through her thoughts. She felt her fingers tapping at imaginary keys. Her mind was not showing her where she needed to go … but instead, the location of her innermost desires.

For it was the music of John Field that was coursing through her mind. She would give anything to hear the master once again. *This* was where she would go if she could — the destination of her ultimate desire. The music drew her like a drug. Not to mention the memory of his lips on her hand. Ah, Mr. Field!

She barely felt the motion of the spaceship, though she knew it was racing through the skies at many times the velocity of a horse-drawn barouche.

Before she could even complete her thought, the spaceship started to descend, making her head spin, then shuddered to a halt.

The bump threw her onto the floor; luckily there was a mass of purple foliage to break her fall.

Welcome to St. Petersburg, said the voice.

23

Mr. Bumbry's Bum

Mrs. Dorrit could not simultaneously worry about her daughters, the gossipy Mrs. Sanditon, *and* the spasms of a poisoned housekeeper. She told Mrs. Sanditon's coachman to urge on the horses and soon found herself at the massive gateway to Flanders House; the chapel was ostentatiously located in plain sight; did these papists have no shame?

Still, the thought of an unshriven housekeeper did not appeal to her sense of order. Summoning up her courage, she descended from the barouche and made her way to the portal. She battered the wooden doors.

No one came. She returned to the coach and bade the driver proceed down the driveway, trying to avert her eyes from the heathen statues that lined the path … though she could not help but notice that none was endowed quite as prodigiously as Monsieur Clatoux.

As she ran up the steps, the doors flew open to reveal an impressive array, a line of servants on either side, ranked in height from little African page to maid to bewigged footman and finally to butler.

"I must speak to His Lordship," said Mrs. Dorrit. "My housekeeper needs a priest. She may die at any moment. Speed is of the essence."

"I see, ma'am," said the butler. "Would not your brother do?"

"I'm afraid not. My housekeeper is ... how can I say it politely ... not a proper member of the Church of England."

"Ah," said the butler. "An Irishwoman." Too late, Mrs. Dorrit noticed the barest hint of brogue beneath his refined tones. He was probably a papist, too, she reflected.

"You're outnumbered, I'm afraid," the butler said. "His Lordship tries to give an opportunity to earn an honest wage to those few of us who survived the persecution of the last few centuries. We didn't *all* get burned at the stake, you know."

"The maids, too?" said Mrs. Dorrit. "And ... those little black fellows? Even *they* are practitioners of your barbaric rites?"

"Oh, no ... they are heathens."

"That's a relief," she said. "At least they have a kind of primal innocence, and have not yet been corrupted by popery."

"In any case," the butler said, "the chaplain of Flanders House is not here."

"And my daughter?" said Mrs. Dorrit. "She is in the library? Tell her to come forthwith."

"Ah — she is — indisposed."

'What? My own daughter? You are keeping her prisoner?"

At that moment, Pauline, her maid-of-all-work, came running out of the hidden hallway that led to the *petite chambre*. She was being pursued by a strapping footman whose wig was askew.

"I could not stop it!" she was screaming. "Ma'am, she's in the library!"

"She's *alone* with the Earl?" Mrs. Dorrit shook with rage. "With a *Roman Catholic?*"

What unspeakable rites was Arabella being subjected to? Though the Earl's lackeys attempted to restrain her, there was no force on Earth that could be stronger than a mother's fury. Shakespeare was wrong: there *is* something more fearsome than a woman scorned. To be frank, Mrs. Dorrit really had no ill will towards papists, and if one were to marry her daughter and had a title, one could surely forgive a little hocus-pocus. But to be so depraved as to be *alone* with Arabella —

She marched through to the back, to the passageway with the *petite chambre*, and beyond it, to one of the hidden doors that led to the library.

What a sight assailed her! This was worse that catching the Earl in mid-liaison. For in a billowing cloud of incense, the Earl and her daughter were standing, hand in hand, facing a *very* young priest, who was at this very moment reciting something in Latin, reading from an open book on a lectern, in a squeaky voice. They were eloping!

Mrs. Dorrit shrieked, ran forwards, and began pummelling the Earl with her fists. "You may be an Earl, my Lord, but you shan't ravish my daughter!"

"My dear Mrs. Dorrit," said His Lordship, "We were

merely trying to circumvent the uncontrollable urge to live in sin."

"Mother, dear, don't make a scene," said Arabella.

"He will trick you into thinking this sham a real marriage, which, in the eyes of the Church of England, it surely is not," said Mrs. Dorrit, "and thus you will be living in sin anyway."

"Oh, we were going to do both ceremonies," said the Earl. "The big one in Mr. Bumbry's church, as befits my station in this village. And this one, for the sake of my immortal soul."

"*Your* soul?" Mrs. Dorrit said, as it dawned on her that this was yet another example of the the masculine gender's unscrupulousness. Heavens, even a Frenchman had more honour! "What about Arabella's?"

"My dear Mama," said Arabella, "my studies in this library have convinced me more than ever that the supreme deity is a creation of men, designed largely to keep us women cooking, cleaning, and dying in childbirth."

Mrs. Dorrit seized the book on the lectern.

"Unhand that book, woman!" said the priest. "It's a thirteenth century illuminated manuscript!" She held the book high and brought it crashing down on the priest's pate. "That is the Holy Vulgate — the word of God!" said the priest.

She beat him about the head and shoulders. "It most certainly is not," she said. "It's not even in English. If the language of Shakespeare and Milton was good enough for Our Lord, it should be good enough for any of you!"

"Oh, please, Mama," Arabella said, "Jesus was a Jew, and spoke Aramaic. And the New Testament is in Greek."

Mrs. Dorrit continued battering the little priest, and presently, still warding off her blows, he scurried out. She pursued him, followed by the Earl and his not-yet-Countess. The priest sprinted through the lobby, where the staff was in confusion, and out the front door. A horse trotted up from behind a statue of Jupiter. The priest leapt on the horse and galloped away.

Mrs. Dorrit stood on the front steps with a priceless illuminated manuscript in her hand, shaking with fury.

"Look what you've gone and done, Mama," said Arabella. "Now we shall have to wait for Mr. Bumbry to perform the rite."

"Roman Catholic priests are hard to come by," the Earl said ruefully. "I wish you had not frightened him off. He is but newly ordained."

Having calmed down a little, Mrs. Dorrit saw that her daughter was in no danger of ravishment; indeed the main question was now to contain the scandal. Indeed, any temporary disparagement by the ton would soon be assuaged when Mrs. Dorrit was able to dominate all of Little Chiswick by being the mother of a Countess.

"You could at least have asked my permission," she said.

"But Mama, I did not wish to delay the consummation for another hour! The Earl is a rake, but really, I don't mind. What little I have seen of his skills bodes well for many enjoyable nights to come. He's already confessed to me all his past amours, and promised to turn over a new leaf. Or at the very least, not to object too much if *I* should take a lover."

Mrs Dorrit gasped. "Sometimes," she said, "I have to say I regret having lived to see the nineteenth century."

"My heartfelt apologies, Mrs. Dorrit. As you know, I've spent the last years amongst savages and slaves. I have very little interest in ceremonies; let's go seek out Mr. Bumbry now, and have *him* do it. Then my darling and I will be able to celebrate our own nocturnal rituals without risking damnation."

"We have a more urgent problem," said Mrs. Dorrit. "My housekeeper is at death's door, and demands a priest of the Roman persuasion."

"We will fetch Mr. Bumbry," said the Earl. "At such a moment as this, I do not think God will be too concerned about the apostolic succession. And in any case, she may be too far gone to notice."

"Time is of the essence," said Mrs. Dorrit.

Mr. Bumbry was not to be found in his office; Mrs. Dorrit had assumed he would be there, poring through some sermon or another. They had entered the church through a back door, to which Mrs. Dorrit had a key.

"Perhaps Mr. Bumbry is in the church itself," Pauline said, but Mrs Dorrit shushed her. She had heard a strange sound coming from within. She could not tell what it was. It sounded like the whimper of a wounded animal.

A door led to the vestry, from which Mr. Bumbry could, via a narrow, curtained entrance, conveniently reach the altar.

Something impelled her to go on tiptoe. Instinctively, she knew she must not make a sound.

The others crowded behind her. Gingerly, she drew the curtain.

The sight that assailed her eyes was one for which

decades of gleeful gossip could never have prepared her.

Behind the altar, Mr. Bumbry was crouching with his haunches in the air, and his trousers about his ankles. He was moaning. That, in fact, was the sound of the wounded animal.

Mr. Bumbry, his face to the cold floor, could not see that he was being watched.

In a gravelly voice, he grunted, "Make haste, the cold cream! See that you apply it liberally!"

As Mrs. Dorrit watched in consternation and, truth to tell, fascination too, Japheth hove into view, approaching Mr. Bumbry with a jar of cold cream in one hand. But this was a Japheth Mrs. Dorrit had never laid eyes on, for he was naked, glistening with sweat, and his engorged weapon was every bit as sizeable as that of Monsieur Clatoux, only it was as black as the latter's was blue.

"My manservant is murdering my brother!" she said in a strangulated whisper.

"My dear Mrs. Dorrit," the Earl said, also in a whisper, "I hardly think so. I have travelled the world, and lived in places far less civilized than Little Chiswick, and I can assure you that Mr. Bumbry is not going to get killed, though there is a species of impalement involved. It seems that your Protestant priests have the same needs as our celibate ones."

"What needs?" Mrs. Dorrit said.

"Oh, bugger," said Miss Arabella, reverting to her sister's unrefined vocabulary.

"Precisely," said the Earl. "I believe we are witnessing an exercise of the vice of Sodom."

Miss Arabella fainted. Pauline giggled. The Earl

watched with a bemused frown.
    Mrs. Dorrit screamed.

24

Piety and Poison

Arabella Dorrit found herself coming to while lying in the lap of the Earl; they were both seated in an exquisitely appointed carriage; Pauline, kneeling on the floor, was holding a vial of smelling salts to her mistress's nose.

She could see through a kind of miasma that ahead of them, her mother was traveling in solitary splendour in an unrecognized barouche; turning, she saw that behind, Japheth was driving the usual second-best coach, while Mr. Bumbry sat alone in the passenger seat, still adjusting his clothing and not meeting anyone's gaze.

"I think I've had quite enough ammonia, Pauline," she said. "I shan't be thinking straight for a week!"

"You will never think straight again, my dear," said the Earl, enveloping her in his arms.

What an afternoon she had had! First, alone in the library for several hours — the presence of Pauline hardly counted — she first managed to plough through several volumes of the Royal Society's journal, finding all sorts of wonders in the writings of one Mr. Herschel: information, for instance, about the moons of the new planet, the one that was supposed to be named *George,* but had had its appellation changed to the somewhat indelicate *Uranus.*

Uranus was, indeed, the grandfather of Jupiter, and the father of Saturn, so it was perhaps more apt that *George,* but at least calling it *George* would have avoided schoolboy sniggering.

She passed the time in a kind of *rêverie,* trying to imagine what sort of creatures the inhabitants of a world named *Uranus* might be. An earthy people for sure, she thought. Then again, she reflected, how could they possibly know that they had been so named by a species that dwelled thousands, nay millions of miles away? After which bodily orifice would they name the inhabitants of Earth? Tush! The natives of that planet must be on a higher plane than mortals. Perhaps they did not even defecate.

Such were her thoughts. Doubtless, her mother would be scandalised that a member of her sex could even conceive of such things, but Arabella saw herself as a modern woman, a true creature of the nineteenth century.

So, when The Right Honourable Tobias David Chrysostom George Mary Durham-St. Aubin-Borgnis, Ninth Earl of Little Chiswick and Viscount Blueborough entered the library of his own stately home, she did not immediately think of it as a compromising situation, merely as an encounter with a rather handsome, slightly dangerous man who happened to have a lot of power.

"Your Lordship!" she said.

"Call me David," he said, as he had before, quite daringly, in public, at the ball.

Arabella said, "Since the last time we met your lips avoided mine by barely a quarter of an inch, I suppose I may, David."

The *frisson* of addressing an Earl by his Christian name made her tingle, but she regained possession of herself within seconds.

"I've thought about nothing but you since the ball," he said.

"I very much doubt that, Your Lordship."

"David."

"Or was it Toby?"

"Anything but Chrysostom. I do abhor that name, and only the Queen calls me that. She does so love to tease; she knew me when I was an infant. It is a punishment for my having made water in her arms when she asked to hold me."

The image of this exalted aristocrat as a baby, urinating on the Queen, was so absurd that Arabella could not help laughing.

"Do laugh again, my dear," said the Earl. "Your laughter drives me to greater distraction than do the amorous whimpers of a thousand women."

"You've only had a thousand?"

"The rest didn't whimper," said the Earl. Such naughty talk! She laughed again and the Earl laughed with her. Here was a male person she felt entirely comfortable with.

She hardly dared to envisage herself a Countess, yet it would certainly allow her to outrank her mother, which might not be a bad thing.

"And I, David, if I whimper, should I be the thousand-and-first? And should I fail to whimper, will I simply be relegated to the unnumbered list of anonymous conquests?"

"You do me wrong, Miss Arabella. You are far more interesting to me than those. I could imagine still being able to converse on interesting topics with you even when we're old! You can talk of astronomy and botany, and you speak more languages even than I, though I don't suppose Mohawk is one of them."

"I daresay not," she said.

"They are quite fascinating, by the way. The Mohawk, I mean.   Did you know that among their kind, it is the women who hold the political power?   Imagine if that were to happen here!"

"Queen Elizabeth I could hardly be said to have been ineffectual," Arabella said.

"Touché!" said the Earl.   "You never give an inch, do you?"

"Never," she said.

"What about eight inches?" the Earl said.

"I hardly think I know what you mean," said Arabella, although she was perfectly cognizant, in a theoretical sort of way, of the male anatomy. "Though eight would be a bit of stretch."

"Ah," said the Earl. "You've never seen one fully extended, then."

"Most certainly not," she said. "My brain is extended, Sir, not my virtue."

"I suppose I shall to propose to you, in that case."

"And I suppose I shall have to accept."

"Luckily, we have a priest on the premises," said His Lordship.

As for the summoning of the priest, the incense wafting through the library, the celerity of the ceremony as the Earl urged the priest to skip the preamble and get on with the vows ... it was all a blur, until the moment Mrs. Dorrit descended like an avenging angel.

Now that the knot had failed to be tied for a moment, Arabella wondered whether the "night of rapture" she had looked forward to would have to be postponed. One of the advantages of eloping would have been that by the time the families found out, it would have been too late to negotiate a dowry, which would have greatly eased the burden for Mrs. Dorrit and her brother. What valuable items yet remained to the Dorrits could all be spent on Anna's instead.

The eccentric assemblage of carriages arrived at the cottage and all alighted, descending upon the front door in various stages of agitation.

When Mrs. Dorrit entered, she found Mrs. O'Keefe sitting comfortably in the drawing-room, and Monsieur had donned one of the late Mr. Dorrit's dressing gowns. So, while unorthodoxly attired, Monsieur was at least decent.

Mrs. Sanditon and Mrs. O'Keefe were gossiping up a storm, behaving almost as though they were social equals, for the housekeeper had the temerity to place herself in Mrs. Dorrit's favourite armchair, rather than stand in attendance as was customary for servants.

On the advent of the party from the church, Mrs. Sanditon rose to take her leave. "Thank you for returning my barouche," she said. "I'd best be going now. So much scandal to spread about the ton! Why, I shall be talked about by all."

Japheth saw her out.

"Don't worry, my dear Mrs. Dorrit," said Monsieur. "I've taken the liberty of erasing her memory."

Well — at least one thing was off her list of stressful things to contemplated. But there were many more.

"The mushrooms were, indeed, poisoned," he continued, "but I've managed to transmute the poison."

"Shall I serve them now?" said Mrs. O'Keefe, reverting to a more servile demeanour. "I'll just run along to the kitchen with Pauline."

And so they were just *en famille:* Mrs. Dorrit, Arabella, Mr. Bumbry, and, if he might be called family, Monsieur Clatoux. And of course the Earl, who might soon become family after all.

"For an old woman," said the Frenchman, "she was certainly enthusiastic during the act of mating; she released enough hormones to save her life."

"Since you say you have erased Mrs. Sanditon's memory, Monsieur," said Mrs. Dorrit, "would you mind not bringing it up anymore?" For she had to admit that she did not much like the idea of sharing Monsieur.

Meanwhile, Mr. Bumbry sat by himself on the pianoforte stool, looking glum.

His Lordship said, "I'm sure *you* want us all to have our memories erased!"

Mr. Bumbry said, "Indeed. Then I could continue to hide my dark secret forever ... as I had to do throughout my childhood, my youth."

"Tosh," Arabella said, "let Uncle have his foibles. I admit I screamed when I saw it, but it's not as though I've never read about it. Plato has plenty to say. There are even scenes in *Fanny Hill* about dark masculine desires. I was but startled; it's not often one sees one's own Uncle being skewered by a manservant."

"Don't take it out on Japheth," said Mr. Bumbry. "After all, he's a slave, and cannot refuse my commands."

"Uncle!" Arabella said. "Didn't you free him?"

Mrs. Dorrit said, "Oh, haven't they *all* been freed yet?"

"Mother, the Slave Act of 1807 didn't *free* anyone; it merely ended the trade."

Mr. Bumbry said, "He's been with us since Lady Chuzzlewit gave him to us because he had outgrown his little pageboy costume. I don't believe there are any papers one way or another."

Arabella said, "Uncle! If you are going to be perpetrating abominations with Japheth, the least you could do is allow him the free will to opt out."

"But he and I have been … ah … you know … for thirty years."

"Free him," Mrs. Dorrit said, "or I'll summon the gossips."

"Very well," said Mr. Bumbry. "Your Lordship will be an official witness." He shouted Japheth's name and the manservant appeared by magic.

Now that she knew that her Uncle and Japheth had been concealing their ungodly behaviour for years, Arabella realized that the relationship would have been perfectly obvious to anyone who was truly looking. For the two of them were constantly communicating with their eyes, with little gestures that one would not notice did one not know. They had a secret language.

"Japheth, my good man," said Mr. Bumbry.   "You're free."

"I know," said Japheth.

"What?" said the Dorrits all at once.

"Her Ladyship free me before she send me to you."

"Do you mean that you have been committing all these *abominations* for decades with Mr. Bumbry," said Mrs. Dorrit, "of your own free will?"

"Well, I have to get *something*," Japheth said.   "I wasn't getting no wages."

"This is all very well," said the Earl, "but I need the Mr. Bumbry to be fully presentable, as we shall soon have a wedding to perform. Now, if possible."

"But," Mrs. Dorrit said, "the beautiful church wedding ... the reception at Flanders House ... surely we will need time to plan an event that the ton will speak of for years to come?"

"Oh, we shall have all that," said His Lordship.   "For show, of course. The church, and the entire spectacle.   I shall even have Tante Charlotte come. However, I would like Mr. Bumbry to perform a private ceremony right now. Surely, as we have just learned, Mr. Bumbry understands the urgency of human longing! If you will not marry us now, Sir, we shall simply commence living in sin."

"Can't have that, can we?" said Mr. Bumbry.   "I'll just fetch my *Book of Common Prayer* from the study."

At that moment, Mrs. O'Keefe came in with the mushroom catsup which was served on little pieces of toast.

Japheth was invited to share the repast as an equal, since

he was not a slave, nor had he been receiving any wages, and thus could not be considered a hired servant, either.

It had been a tiring day. From her exciting encounter with the Earl, to Mrs. O'Keefe's poisoning, to the discovery that her uncle was secretly practising vices in the church, to the revelation that their manservant had never actually *been* a servant ... Arabella did not think she could survive any more drama. She bit down on some mushroom-topped toast. It was delicious. In fact, they must all have been hungry, because the food was gone almost instantly; the ladies in particular showed a very unladylike gusto.

At that moment, Pauline came running into the room. "Monsieur!" she cried. "Your spaceship is gone — and Miss Anna along with it!"

Mrs. Doritt began laughing uncontrollably. Mr. Bumbry and Japheth were giggling. What could be so funny about a missing spaceship?

It was then that Arabella saw that Mrs. Dorrit was turning into a blue camel. Japheth had wings, and was hovering in the air. Mr. Bumbry was wearing an exquisite lady's gown. And Arabella herself, looking down at her hands, saw that they had turned into the paws of an ape. She too began laughing. What madness was this?

"Perhaps I should clarify! I took out the poison," said Monsieur, "but I didn't remove the hallucinogens."

25

My Big Fat English Wedding

Mrs. Dorrit decided it was time to call a family meeting. After all, although Mr. Bumbry was the titular head of the clan, he would obviously not be any use in any discussion of *what was to be done.* He had, after all, been *doing* a little too much already.

The family meeting would have to include everyone who *knew* anything, and yet also be so secretive that not a word of what was to be discussed could be allowed to leak into boudoirs of the ton's various gossips; for each of the family members was now possessed of a Dark Secret, and each stood to lose — or *gain* — everything, were the pieces to fall *exactly* into place.

The meeting would therefore have to be in a place where

no decent person would willingly set foot — a place no one even knew existed.

Luckily, the Earl had such a place.

It had begun life as a priest's hole — that is to say, a secret room in Flanders House where a priest would be able to say mass, during the time of the persecutions of Catholics — the dark times (well, they were of course *not* dark times for Protestants) when hundreds of Catholics were hanged, drawn and quartered during the 1570s.

It was quite a cloak-and-dagger operation to get to the room, for even His Lordship's servants were not entirely cognizant of the hole's location. In fact, Mrs. Dorrit was met at the door by one footman, who led her to the space beneath the sweeping staircase, the one that led to both the *petite chambre* and the library. From the library, a bookcase swung out when you tweaked the nose of a bust of the Emperor Augustus, revealing a passageway.

A different footman directed Mrs. Dorrit down a steep and winding stairwell, at the bottom of which His Lordship himself was there to lead her through the last corridor, which ended in a room that had surely once been a dungeon.

"Heavens, Your Lordship!" said Mrs. Dorrit. "Am I to be imprisoned?"

"Hardly, my dear mother-in-law," said the Earl.

Mrs. Dorrit felt a surge of warmth at being so addressed by no less a figure than an Earl, albeit a papist. "Why, my dear —" She suddenly realized she did not quite know what to call him. For "Your Lordship" would now surely seem to formal, yet she was unaware of which of the plethora of Christian names he possessed was the one he actually went by. "My dear son-in-law," she finished, erring on the side of caution.

"This room is not a dungeon at all. Indeed, during the troubles, we would sometimes pretend to imprison a Jesuit or other so-called heretic here in accordance with the 1571 treason statute, whilst allowing him secret knowledge of the way out. Which I shall show you myself, now."

The wall in the back of the dungeon gave way with pressure on a protruding brick. There was another stairway down to a kind of antechamber with half a dozen doors, suggesting many alternative routes to reach this hideaway.

None of the six doors led to their destination. Nay, rather, it was the fireplace, which was large enough to crawl into — odd for an antechamber so cramped. But when the Earl took a poker from the stand in front, and used it to prod a few protuberances in the back wall, that, too, slid open, and he stepped into an area behind the fireplace. He held out his hand for Mrs. Dorrit, who gingerly followed, crouching and lifting her skirts instinctively to avoid soot, though the fireplace looked as though it had never seen a fire.

The meeting room was far more impressive than she could have imagined, despite having no windows. There was a fine carved oak table and chairs that were in fine condition, considering that they appeared to be at least of Tudor origin, if not older. The room was well-lit, with lamps on sconces on the walls, and was relatively cool as well, even drafty; some ventilation seemed to come from above.

It seemed that Mrs. Dorrit was the last one to arrive.

The Earl escorted her to a seat that was opposite to his

own. To Mrs. Dorrit's right sat Monsieur Clatoux; to her left, the wayward Mr. Bumbry. On the Earl's left was Miss Arabella, and there was an empty seat for Miss Anna.

Not at the main table, as befit their social status, and sitting on stools rather than chairs, were the family help: Mrs. O'Keefe, Pauline, and Japheth.

"Is it absolutely necessary to have the servants here?" said Mr. Bumbry.

"Uncle," said Arabella, "they've *seen* things."

"Precisely, said the Earl. They shall participate in this conversation. I don't see how you can object to Japheth's insertion into this discussion, Mr. Bumbry. You don't seem to have objected to his insertions elsewhere."

The maid and the housekeeper giggled.

Mr. Bumbry looked as though he would shrivel up into the chair. "Oh, I've sinned, I've sinned," he sighed.

"Oh, nonsense," said the Earl. "You've done nothing more than the entire male aristocracy of England did at Eton."

Mrs. Dorrit realized she had better take charge, before the meeting became a chaos of bickering and recrimination. "All of you, listen! The name of our family shall *not* be dragged through the mud. Not when we stand at the brink of dominating the entire ton. But this is a time for absolute truth. We must face our problems squarely, taking, as it were, the bull by the horns. We shall not leave this room until we have a clear plan that will put us all above reproach — and more importantly, above the Mrs. Sanditons and their ilk, who thrive on the destruction of reputations while having no redeeming qualities of their own."

"In that case," said Mr. Bumbry, "let's start with my own, ah, peccadilloes."

"No, we shall not," said Mrs. Dorrit firmly. "If, as His Lordship indicates, you're merely indulging in a practice known by all Old Etonians, I daresay we shall get away with never mentioning it at all."

"Indeed," said the Earl, "that is how it is dealt with in all proper institutions of education."

"I see. Don't ask, don't tell, is it?" Arabella said, seeming pleased to have come up with such an original new turn of phrase.

"That maxim has served the aristocracy well for a thousand years," said the Earl. "It's such a shame that the middle classes have become so bloody *moral.* Things were a lot better when there weren't any middle classes at all."

"Then it is a shame that I'm just a simple country parson, and thus burdened with a conscience," said Mr. Bumbry. "Oh, I've agonized, I've battled my base desires, attempted to conquer the desires of the flesh by all sorts of mortification … Japheth knows. Many a time, I've had him try to whip the sin from me, only to discover that I rather enjoyed the whipping."

Mrs. Dorrit was getting rather irritated by her brother's self-pity. He had been a lot more entertaining when he was breathing fire and brimstone and anti-popery. This meek new incarnation was a little disappointing.

"A simple elevation of status should make our sins disappear," said the Earl. "The main thing is not to be perceived as middle class. I'm sure there's a bishopric available."

"What?" said Mr. Bumbry, suddenly interested.

"I said a bishopric!" said the Earl. "Perhaps you heard something a tad more titillating?"

"Oh, right," said Mr. Bumbry, descending once more into a miasma of gloom.

"We shall have the King set you up as soon as possible," said the Earl. "After all, Tante Charlotte adores your whole family."

"Well, then, Arabella," Mrs. Dorrit said, "what about you?"

Miss Arabella said, "I've done nothing more than what any red-blooded, passionate woman dreams of. I'm far more concerned about my sister… and about Monsieur. We have used his powers so much for our personal gain, that he is weakening. He *must* be facilitated in his urgent need to telephone home."

Mrs. Dorrit said, "And what exactly is telephoning? And are we not already home?"

Monsieur said, "There is a device I must create. I had been putting it all together on my ship … and apparently all I need is to bring it to the mechanical exhibition in London, where there is a contraption I can use to set it in motion…."

The Earl said, "So, we need to get your vehicle back from wherever it has carried Miss Anna to."

Monsieur said, "If I know Miss Anna, she has almost certainly gone to Russia."

"Of course," Arabella said. "John Field."

"More royal intervention needed," said the Earl. "We shall have Tante Charlotte invite him to England to give a concert."

"She would do that?" said Arabella.

"Most assuredly," said the Earl. "When she first became Queen, she even had little Mozart to the palace for a recital."

"It would be the most exclusive soirée of all time," Mrs. Dorrit said. "That could certainly create a distraction."

"There is an even greater distraction we shall provide," said the Earl. "Every scandal ever to stain your escutcheon will be wiped out. The soirée, even with the King and Queen *and* Mr. Field, the greatest English composer of our time, will be eclipsed by the greatest spectacle ever to be seen in Little Chiswick. I am referring, of course, to my wedding … and the ball that will follow, which my Tante Charlotte will doubtless wish to host at the Queen's own private retreat, Buckingham House — which is not too far from the Mechanical Exhibition, giving Monsieur a chance to communicate with his Frenchmen in space."

"My dear," Arabella said sweetly, "you seem to have forgotten that we're already married. Indeed … dare I say it openly … we have … consummated."

"Enough!" said Mrs. Dorrit, though secretly she was delighted at the prospect of perhaps becoming the grandmother of an Earl. "You plan to add bigamy to our list of scandals?"

"Mother dear," said Arabella, "bigamy is when you marry two women at once … not when you marry the same woman twice. Besides, no one knows. As far as the world is concerned, only one wedding will have taken place."

"It will be the talk of the century," said the Earl. "For the fact that I will marry Arabella in the Church of England, and have the sacrament administered by no less a figure than the newly appointed Bishop Bumbry … will signify to all and sundry not *just* the supreme ennoblement of the Dorrits … but also that I, The Right Honourable Tobias David Chrysostom George Mary Durham-St. Aubin-Borgnis, Ninth Earl of Little Chiswick and Viscount Blueborough, shall have become, to all intents and purposes —"

"A *Protestant!*" Mrs. Dorrit gasped.

"A miracle!" said Mr. Bumbry under his breath. "Why, the conversion of the Little Chiswicks would, indeed, be the gossip of the century."

"Conversion?" said Arabella. "I doubt that David *actually* believes in anything at all."

"Jesus, Mary, and Joseph!" Mrs. O'Keefe sighed. There was a mighty crash as she fell from her stool.

"She's fainted," said Japheth.

26

A Primitive Mode of Transport

As Pauline and Japheth attempted to revive Mrs. O'Keefe, Arabella Dorrit slowly came to the realization that the fate of her entire family had fallen upon her slender shoulders.

"You, Mother," she said to Mrs. Dorrit, "must of course help to plan the festivities. The guest list, the musicians, the delicacies to be served — and all in collaboration with Her Majesty. This will take an entire month, I am sure, and will be a magnificent capstone to the season."

Her mother said, "And His Lordship the Earl of Little Chiswick —"

"David," said His Lordship. "Or Toby, if you prefer. Anything but Chrysostom. If you call me that, I shall have you put in the stocks."

"Don't be silly, David," Arabella said. "Earls don't sentence people to the stocks anymore. This is the nineteenth century!"

Mrs. O'Keefe was muttering something about suet puddings.

"She's raving, Missus," said Japheth to Mrs. Dorrit.

"My dear mother-in-law," said the Earl, "you shall leave the ball to my aunt, and the wedding to me — as soon as we have figured out which bishopric is available for Mr. Bumbry."

"It therefore seems," said Arabella, "that the heftiest job has probably fallen to me, hasn't it? I mean — the job of making sure that my sister, Mr. Field, and the Frenchman's spaceship arrive in time for the wedding."

"I shall need a number of things from the ship," said Monsieur, "if I am to enable this spectacle to be as splendiferous as I think your inchoate human imaginations have attempted to conceive."

"So we must straight away to St. Petersburg — assuming of course that that is where my sister has landed — present the invitation to Mr. Field, who as a guest of His Imperial Majesty might need to obtain royal permission to depart — and then we must return here in time to build Monsieur's device, bring it to the Mechanical Exhibition, and summon his fellow Frenchmen," Miss Arabella said.

"I suppose we'd best be off, then," said Monsieur Clatoux.

His Lordship said, "My dear Monsieur, I don't think you realize that it will take some time to get to St. Petersburg. Even the fastest ship, at eighteen hundred nautical miles and flying like the wind at four to six knots, would take —

"

"About three weeks," Arabella said.

"Weeks?" Monsieur said in alarm. "What exactly are *weeks?"*

Arabella said, "Why, Monsieur, a week is seven revolutions of our planet on its axis." Not for nothing had she pored over those astronomical textbooks!

"Ah." Monsieur Clatoux thought for a moment. "About seventeen quintillion *bzmakzplati.* We'll never make it."

"But it will take but a few moments to return," Arabella said.

"Assuming they *are* in St. Petersburg," said Monsieur Clatoux forlornly. "Assuming my ship is there. Assuming the ship is in working order, and Miss Anna was not somehow gummed up its drive. Assuming that Mr. Field can get the Tsar's permission. Assuming —"

"My dear Monsieur," said Mr. Bumbry. "Are we not desperate enough already, without your *assumptions?* Let us rather trust in God."

Arabella was a little nonplussed that her uncle was even saying anything, seeing as he had been caught indulging in what was generally regarded as unspeakable vice. On the other hand, the Earl himself was simply shrugging it off as something *everyone* did at Eton. Mr. Bumbry had seemed chastened for the last few days, but now he was speaking of God. "Is that not a tad hypocritical, uncle?"

"By no means, my dear," said Mr. Bumbry. "I have a chance to reflect on God's true nature, and I understand now that God is love. And that even my obscure fumblings with our manservant were not born of malice, but out of a kind of affection. I am sure I shall be forgiven in time — as all of us must be."

"Ha!" said the Earl. "He will make a sterling bishop! He will convince us all that black is white!"

"Hasn't convinced me, sir," said Japheth.

Once again, Arabella Dorrit was poised to travel far beyond the confines of the ton. The first time had been a trip orchestrated by Monsieur, a journey through time and space that had done a great deal to restore the wits of His Majesty.

"This time, alas," said Monsieur, "we shall not be travelling in comfort."

Indeed, their journey to the Port of London was decidedly déclassé, with only one servant, the much put-upon Japheth, forced to carry all their luggage. They had taken a coach from Little Chiswick at the exorbitant rate of tuppence per mile, per passenger, though Japheth, as a servant, was only charged half.

Luckily, Arabella's secret husband had provided them not only with a generous amount of gold, but a letter of credit that could be presented at any bank in Europe. The Earl had contrived to book them passage on a vessel bound for Copenhagen. Thence, Arabella and the Monsieur would continue on to St. Petersburg. Three weeks did not seem too horrid a span, but Arabella's stomach began to churn from almost the very first minute.

Indeed, she spent seven or eight days tossing and turning in her quarters, only leaving to vomit. The sea was decidedly unpleasant. The sailors avoided her, disturbed, perhaps, that a woman should be there at all. When they did stop to look, they stared, drooling like predators.

Monsieur, on the other hand, was having a grand time; he had the knack for regaling strangers with stories. It was good that his audience did not believe them.

Apart from the constant heaving over the side, therefore, Arabella's remembrance of the first week was something of a blur. Sleeping and regurgitating were her main occupations.

She had vague recollections of a peg-legged captain regaling the guests, and of Monsieur stripping to prove to the sailors that he was, indeed, blue all the way down.

And of course, more vomiting.

Putting in at Copenhagen for a day, Arabella had the chance to try some of their smørrebrød, as the locals called their fermented bread piled high with incongruous toppings. It was indeed as chaotic a concoction as it sounded, and she yearned for the homely comfort of an eel pie.

But further into the Baltic Sea, Miss Arabella realized she was no longer quite as nauseated. Indeed, when she appeared on deck she was no longer staggering. Indeed, she was beginning to feel lulled by the smooth rocking of the ship, and the odd squeaks and groans of settling wood and snoring seamen.

It was a clear night. The moon was full. Stars sparkled and Arabella did not think she had seen anything quite so beautiful. She could easily make out glowering Betelgeuse in the shoulder of Orion. Suddenly, a shower of meteors flashed. She shuddered with delight. What it must be to actually study such phenomena, instead of fussing over the appropriate length of a pelisse!

It seemed next that the entire ocean was rumbling. Then there was a series of eerie, high-pitched keening sounds.

What creature could make such sounds?

In the distance, beneath the moon, a whale was breaching.

She thrilled at the sight.

And then she realized that the wailing was a duet. Other moans were coming from ... the fo'c'sle of this very ship! And there was Monsieur Clatoux, crooning, gurgling, and making deep growling sounds, matching the whale song note for note!

Bemused, Arabella watched for some time. The whale, a humpback she thought, approached the ship and the dialogue continued for sometime. At length, the creature leapt up in a tremendous arc, sounded with a thunderous splash, and there was silence save for the quiet ripple of the ocean.

Monsieur turned to Arabella with a sigh and let himself down from the fo'c'sle. He seemed more serene, more at peace.

"Why did you make those noises?" asked Arabella.

"Noises? Oh ... you mean ... I was conversing. She told me a great deal."

"The whale? What could a whale have to say to you?"

For Arabella knew of whales only as the source of corsets and lamp oil.

"Why, I've had a more profound conversation that I've had in six months in Little Chiswick. One spends so much time amongst humans, it is easy to forget that there *are* genuinely sentient beings on your planet," said Monsieur.

"Profound? But what did you speak of?"

"You would not have understood it, my dear."

Only then, perhaps, did Arabella understand the gulf

between them. And only then did she have an inkling of the terrible loneliness he must feel. For despite all this talk of France, it was she who truly understood that Monsieur came from the stars.

"We shall build your telephone, Monsieur," she said. "I swear it."

27

Hope and Harpoon

Arabella returned to the deck at dawn to discover Monsieur Clatoux still, apparently, deep in conversation with the whale; for a succession of chirps, whistles, and rumblings emerged from his unopened lips.

"Ah," he said, "Miss Arabella. I trust you have regenerated successfully?"

"I have slept reasonably well," she said, considering the ceaseless motion of these waves, and the gnawing knowledge that, given our current circumstances, we actually do not have quite enough time to fullfil our mission before disaster strikes."

In fact, it was with great sorrow that she considered the options for poor Monsieur Clatoux. He had sacrificed his very flesh and blood (or whatever passed for such bodily essences in France) for the salvation of the Dorrits' good name — a sacrifice not unlike that of Our Lord himself for the redemption of all humanity.

"Yes, Monsieur," she said, "I am troubled. You have done so much for us, and at such cost; I *must* find a way to bring you back to yourself. Oh, my inability to save you … it is intolerable, Monsieur!"

"On my world," said Monsieur, "we are infinitely patient. We don't allow little things like mortality to disturb our *sang-froid*."

At that he began to commune with the whale again. At length, he said, "I believe we have found a way to arrive in St. Petersburg with greater celerity. Our friend will help us."

"Our friend?"

"Our cetacean friend, Miss Arabella."

The whale was approaching their ship. As it came closer, Arabella realized it was enormous; indeed, it dwarfed the ship itself.

"I pray, do not be afraid," said Monsieur. "My friend finds your fear unappetising."

"Unappetising?"

"Fear fills the air with certain, ah, *pheromones*. I'm not sure whether your culture knows of this word. It is why animals know fear. It is the reason why, whenever you are in close propinquity with one such as myself, you begin to enter a lubricious state."

"I'm sure I don't know what you mean," Arabella said, though what he said made her shudder to the very core.

"Come with me now. Suppress your terror."

He extended a blue hand. Nervously, Arabella took it. He heaved her up and stepped towards larboard, then began to clamber up what seemed to be the empty air. "It is a forcefield," he said. "It is perfectly safe, but only for a few minutes; I cannot sustain it long."

He tugged her arm and pulled her along and presently, she was actually walking above the waves! Several sailors were on deck, and they were watching in awe as Arabella and the Frenchman superambulated the ocean and arrived on the whale's flank. Oddly, though there was a high wind, Arabella neither felt the wind nor smelt the salt tang of it, nor heard the cries of circling gulls; it seemed that they were enveloped in a kind of tunnel of nothingness. She was used to the miraculous by now.

Perhaps Our Lord was a Frenchman, she thought. *After all, He did walk over the Sea of Galilee!*

They landed on the whale's back. It was like an island — a wobbly one, to be sure, afflicted by little tremors or earthquakes. From a distance it had seemed smoothly grey, but standing on the surface of Leviathan, Miss Arabella could see that the skin was coated with barnacles and bits of seaweed and other detritus of the deep.

"You will need to brace yourself, my dear," said Monsieur. "We are going to be travelling at considerable velocity, the straightest possible path towards the Russian coast."

The whale started to accelerate, but it was considerably more smooth than the ride on the boat. "This is splendid!" Arabella said, reflecting that Nature in her infinite wisdom and variety was able to produce movement far more graceful than the pitch and yaw of a precarious wooden bucket tossing in the sea.

"Hold my arm tightly," said Monsieur. I am attached to the whale's flank by a protoplasmic adhesion which I've managed by extending some pseudopods subcutaneously into our friend, here. But she is in no pain, I assure you; there is a lot of protective blubber."

Monsieur Clatoux's stream of polysyllabic discourse filled Arabella with an almost sensual satisfaction. Why couldn't Englishmen sound so intellectual? For a moment, Arabella even contemplated whether she would dare to … enter into some kind of union with this creature. What a sinful thought!

"I'm sure your husband would not mind,"said Monsieur. "No, I am not reading your thoughts, merely exercising my heightened olfactory abilities to be able to analyze the complex aromas of arousal your glands are producing."

Why, Arabella thought, such talk was a thrilling as her husband's touch! She shuddered with guilt.

"You would not be betraying him with another man, after all. For I am hardly that. I am, indeed, not even of this Earth."

So saying, he embraced her, and their lips joined in a heady osculation that felt, to Miss Arabella, like volcanoes, or fireworks. At length, she broke away. "You may not be a man," she said, "but you could certainly stand in for one, at a pinch!"

He laughed, and they kissed once more, as the waves surged around them and they sped through the waters. Definitely, Arabella thought, something I shall not be telling my husband.

But at that moment their tender solitude was shattered. A massive shaft came flying through the air and lanced the whale's side.

Arabella screamed.   There was another ship coming alongside, and the whale had been struck by a harpoon.

Dark blood was gushing from the wound. Three boats, with rowers and more men with weapons, were rapidly approaching.

"Our friend will have to sound," said Monsieur.

"But we shall drown!"

"No! She will hide us within her very bowels!"

So saying, Monsieur waved with his hands once more, generating another force-field, this one evidently a bubble rather than a bridge. "Hold on very tightly, my dear Miss Arabella!" he gasped. They were flying through the air, flung skyward by the flap of a fin. The whale leapt. They soared. The whale uttered a tremendous bellow, seeming to shake the very sea.

The ball of force that held them flew like a cricket ball. The whale seemed suspended, defying Mr. Newton's *Law of Universal Gravitation* entirely. Then she opened her capacious mouth and the force-bubble fell onto her tongue.

It was completely dark, but Arabella could tell that they were sliding down some slick, slimy tunnel.

Abruptly, they were turned in a topsy-turvy direction and the whale was now sounding rapidly, racing down into the depths. Arabella's stomach churned.

"We shall die!" Arabella shrieked.

"My dear Miss Arabella," said Monsieur, "even an alien such as myself has read your tales of Jonah and Leviathan. We have plenty of air. I shall render the bubble slightly permeable, so that we can partake of any stray oxygen that happens to be in this gullet."

"*What was that?*" A torrent of — something — washed over them.

"Oh, just plankton," said Monsieur.

They were now moving up and down as the wounded whale swam like a demon, trying to dislodge the harpoon and outrun the whalers.

Like any imaginative woman, Miss Arabella had often imagined her own death. But never had she imagined she might expire within the belly of a sea-monster. Fortunately, she had tightened her corsets that morning, so she was able to avoid the full horror of her own demise by conveniently fainting.

28

A Wife for the Tsar

Since the Frenchman's vehicle crash-landed in the gardens of the Imperial Palace in St Petersburg, Miss Anna had spent every waking moment in the company of the man she most admired, John Field, the greatest composer of his generation. Not, mind you, as one who receives a man's amorous attentions; nay, rather, as an admirer of great music, as a disciple.

Spending all this time with a man would not have been possible within the confines of the ton, but this was Russia, where wanton licentiousness was practically *de rigeur.*

Russia, a thousand times the size of Little Chiswick, where no one knew Miss Anna, and no one judged her, for the Russians are a people ruled entirely by their passions, and not capable of refined English logic. Why, they drank vodka instead of tea!

And while Mr. Field's nocturnes were fully informed with the sweetness and gentility of their Englishness, his music also contained a kind of surging savagery beneath that exterior. No wonder he was so beloved in Russia!

And no wonder Miss Anna herself adored him, or at least his music; for she knew now that beneath her plain exterior throbbed a passion as potent as that which imbued those nocturnes.

Then there were the soirées, which were like nothing in Little Chiswick. For one thing, these people completely lacked the kind of decorum that would be proper to an English event. The displays of minks, sables, diamonds, rubies, the tiaras, the necklaces, the gigantic earrings that must have rendered deportment an almost Herculean task for the average *grande dame,* were *de rigueur.* Luckily, all conversation at such events was carried on in French, so Miss Anna was at least able to interject from time to time.

Now, back at home, one did on occasion speak French, *for French does add a frisson of sophistication to a conversation,* Miss Anna thought. But did these people have to actually attempt to speak it *properly?* They acted as if they actually spoke the language naturally, rather than simply affecting a veneer of continental culture to impress each other. Didn't they have their own language?

Well, of course they did, insofar as such a hodgepodge of gliding vowels and crunching consonantal clusters could be called a language. But Miss Anna noted that this was a tongue the aristocracy only used with members of the lower classes.

Mr. Field moved in exalted circles indeed, and was frequently summoned to play his nocturnes for the His Imperial Majesty himself. On such occasions, she would accompany her mentor, attending him as his appointed page-turner. Which was indeed an honor that Anna could scarcely credit; in England, she should not have felt worthy enough to untie his shoelaces.

But here in St. Petersburg, all things were possible.

Even a veiled suggestion from Tsar Alexander….

"Mademoiselle Anna," he had said to her over tea, "perhaps I might extend to you an offer of an … ah … arrangement?"

"Oh!" said Anna. "You do me great honor, Your Imperial Majesty."

"Perhaps tonight?" said the Tsar.

"You have a particular song in mind?" she said. "Perhaps a Russian folk song?" She imagined herself arranging one of those pretty pentatonic ditties for the pianoforte, with a delicate filigree of arpeggios accentuated by lush harmonies.

"I am not sure what you mean," said the Tsar. "It must be your imperfect French. You desire to serenade me before I … ah … perform the act? *Charmante!*"

"What song?" said Miss Anna. "I pray it be a sinuous and mellifluous one, yet easy on the fingers."

"I see! *Les doigts et la bouche!* You shall perform both the, ah, manual and oral arrangements?" said His Majesty. "I hardly expected such wild abandon amongst the English."

"Perhaps," she said, "it is because your brilliant long summer"white nights" have made me lightheaded."

That afternoon, His Imperial Majesty had decreed an alfresco feast. On the Embankment Side of the Winter Palace, a platform had been raised so that the guests could observe traffic on the Neva. They were to hear a recital by a ten-year-old prodigy from Poland, a boy named Szopen, or Szopinski, who would play a few mazurkas and polonaises whilst the aristocrats were sinfully suffering a surfeit of sevruga.

At the main table, Mr. Field sat across from Miss Anna, and His Imperial Majesty himself sat upon a golden throne. There was another throne for the Tsarina, but the Empress was absent, as indeed she always seemed to be; Miss Anna was not absolutely certain she had seen her at all since her sojourn began.

The boy played with aplomb. "What do you think, Mr. Field?" said the Emperor.

"Bit of a showoff," said Mr. Field.

She watched the boy's fingers fly with astonishing celerity across the keys. Mr. Field was far too English to betray such vulgarity even in the throes of passion. Russians, Poles … what was it about them?

The boy's piece came to a thundering close and the Tsar leapt to his feet. "Bravo!" he cried, and actually left his seat to go and give the child a mighty pat on the shoulder.

"His Imperial Majesty is in quite the good mood," said Mr. Field.

"Indeed. Perhaps it's because I am to make an 'arrangement' for him," she said. "I am to call upon His Majesty tonight."

"Alone?"

"I hardly think so. The Tsar rarely has fewer than twenty minions lurking in the shadows."

"Ah."

"I wonder what song he wishes me to arrange."

At that, Mr. Field began to laugh uproariously. "I knew the Tsar's English was bad, my dear Miss Anna, but I didn't realize yours was as well!"

"Whatever do you mean?"

"Did you honestly think that His Imperial Majesty wanted you to create a piano version of some Russian folk song? Perhaps ..." he giggled again. "Perhaps '*Yo, heave ho?*' That would leave little to the imagination! *Yeshcho razik, yeshcho da raz!* That is to say, Once more, once again, still once more!"

"Again? What again?" said Anna, even more befogged than before.

"You have been invited to an *arrangement,* my dear Miss Dorrit, because His Imperial Majesty already has a wife. Alas, she is busy running the country, so *arrangements* are necessary. In French, they call it *concubinage.*"

The truth hit her like a thunder-stroke. "He is willing to countenance my ruin? That I should be so compromised!"

"Russians, dear madam, do not compromise at all, I'm afraid. More than *compromised* ... you would be possessed ... ravished ... utterly penetrated, if you know what I mean."

"I'm sure I don't."

"Perhaps it will be easier for you to comprehend if I simply refer to what is about to happen to you as *a fate worse than death.*"

"*Mon dieu*, Mr. Field! I must depart instantly!"

"Leave the presence of the Tsar of all the Russias without a written Imperial Permission?"

"Well, I didn't exactly *come* here with permission, did I?"

Immensely agitated, Anna rose from her seat, flinging her arms with such abandon that she pulled off the tablecloth. A bowl of caviar flew into the air and landed on her head. She screamed.

The Tsar returned at that very moment, his arm around the shoulders of the beaming prodigy. "I daresay Szopinski will become even more famous than you one day, Mr. Field! We'll have to start calling him *Chopin,* though." he said. "And, Mademoiselle," he continued, bearing down on the still ululating Anna, "you must be terribly excited about tonight!"

"I most certainly am *not!*" Miss Anna snorted.

So there they stood: the Emperor, shocked at having his will thwarted; Miss Anna, shocked at learning that an arrangement was a code word for an assignation; and Mr. Field, consumed by the comedy of the situation.

At that moment, the River Neva erupted.

Boatmen were screaming. The water was churning and heaving. A kind of geyser exploded out of the maelstrom. Was it an earthquake? No! Something *huge* was emerging from the foam. It was not a ship. It was larger. It was a smooth hill covered with leather, with tiny eyes and yawning jaws.

It was a whale!

And, squeezing himself out from within the whale's blowhole, was Monsieur Clatoux, who was now attempting to pull Miss Arabella out! A gust of wet air propelled them out. They were sputtering.

Ascending with the fountain, Monsieur and Arabella floated into the air, somersaulted, and made a soft landing on the grounds of the Imperial Embankment!

"Ah, Monsieur Nicolai," the Tsar said, as Monsieur bowed deeply.

"Good to see you, Nicolai!" said Mr. Field.

The whale backed out of the Neva and headed back toward the harbour.

"You don't seem too taken aback by my curious mode of transport, Sasha," said Monsieur to the Emperor, who seemed not a bit perturbed by the Frenchman's use of an intimate nickname.

"Whales visit the Embankment from time to time," said the Emperor. "Usually when they mate, for the position of their amorous congress is so unstable that the female, on her back, must swim at considerable speed; her mate then, as it were, overshoots and lands in the river. Slava visits me frequently." he added, "though he rarely carries passengers. Not live ones, at any rate."

"This one isn't Slava," said the Frenchman, "it's his wife."

"Oh well. All whales look alike," said the Emperor.

"You're just in time," Anna said, embracing her sister. "I was almost ruined tonight!"

"There now," Arabella said soothingly. "All will be well if we accomplish our mission."

Arabella drew from her bosom a damp missive. She unfolded it and handed it to Mr. Field. "Your presence is required at a Royal Command performance at a wedding in

the presence of Their Majesties," she said, trying to un-
wrinkle the epistle as he unsealed it.

"It's tomorrow," Monsieur Clatoux said. "There's no
time to be lost. So, Miss Anna, where have you mislaid my
spaceship?"

29

Alien and Onion

Since The return to Little Chiswick was as uneventful as the departure had been arduous. For Monsieur's spaceship remained where it had landed, in the gardens of the Winter Palace near the apartments of Mr. Field. With Monsieur back in control, things were simple and the journey was more or less instantaneous. Mr. Field had little time for wonderment, since they had already arrived by the time he managed to say anything.

What he said was a *most* unbecoming, "Well, I'll be damned!" This was the kind of profanity more likely to come Miss Anna's lips than from a respected composer, Arabella thought.

Around the witching hour, then, Mr. Field and Miss Anna were disgorged in front of the vicar's cottage. "Now,

Miss Arabella," said Monsieur with the gravest urgency, "before we depart on our mission to save your family — and my life — I need you to go inside and ask Mrs. O'-Keefe for some bulbous plants of the species *Allium cepa.*"

"You require onions, Monsier? Whatever for?"

"We need a supply of *syn-Propanethial-S-oxide*, Miss Arabella, a substance that, in your world, is released only by the squeezing of an onion."

She obtained the onions and returned to the spaceship. "There is not much time," said Monsieur. "I am weakening." Miss Arabella and Monsieur continued their journey and arrived almost immediately at the Mechanical Exhibition.

The Exhibition, on Tichborne Street, near the Haymarket, was not of course open at this hour. Or, indeed, at *any* hour these days, for the public had lost interest and it was only reopened on occasion, for the odd tour of a Ladies' Society, or a class from the local grammar-school. Arabella herself knew of it only by repute.

The spaceship's arrival elicited little comment from the onlookers; the streets were not exactly thronging. There was a little bit of light, for a single gas lamp, installed at the turn of the century as a testament to the new century's enormous scientific prowess, cast a soft yellow glare in the alley where they landed.

A shabbily dressed woman, perhaps one of the legendary ladies of ill fame of whom Arabella had heard spoken in dire whispers, shrieked and ran off; then the two of them were alone.

The telephonic device that Monsieur had crafted was built around a battered velocipede. Arabella and Monsieur wheeled it down the alley and reached the façade of the Exhibition, a modestly impressive exemplar of the architecture of the Age of Enlightenment.

The portal was locked, of course, but Monsieur simply made his finger very long and slim, and pushed it in the keyhole; he concentrated a moment, letting his flesh flow into the correct nooks and crannies, and the door creaked open; he withdrew his finger and Arabella noted that it was now shaped exactly like a key … for a few moments … before metamorphosing back into a finger.

They stepped into a huge, dusty, ghostly hall, pulling the contraption inside.

Miss Arabella found a lamp, and lit it; with the help of its glow she located and lit a few others. The chamber, cavernous and gloomy, was now illumined with an eerie, flickering light.

Suddenly, a cuckoo called. Arabella gasped.

The bird flew across the ceiling before landing at her feet. She picked it up and saw that it was a creature made of metal, triggered by some mechanism that had sensed her footsteps on the marble floor.

"Oh!" she said, embarrassed to have been frightened.

She turned to Monsieur. "But Monsieur Clatoux: how, oh how," she said, "are we going to get your device to do what you need done?"

They surveyed the various contraptions in the dim light.

There were numerous clocks. None were running, for each needed to be wound. Unable to resist, she walked up to the nearest one and turned a key. A few more cuckoo calls, and a silver angel began to turn on the head of a spike. She turned another and music sounded, petering out after a few bars.

In the middle of the hall was a mysterious, mountainous object covered by a tarp. Perhaps this was the machine which would restore Monsieur.

"I shall endeavour to explain," said Monsieur. "You see, this meteorite which you so kindly managed to purloin from the town hall in Little Chiswick is not of this Earth. It is in fact a lump of material that might be called, I suppose, 'extra-terrestrial' — and as such it contains something very useful to me indeed: a colony of dysprosium-fixing bacteria."

"I see," said Arabella, trying to sound intelligent.

"You needn't pretend to understand," said the Frenchman. "I myself am no expert, but have only the knowledge of a layman in these matters."

"I see," said Arabella again. "I myself have no knowledge of for example, the physics of combustion, yet I know how to operate a stove. That's what you're saying, I suppose." Explaining a gas lamp or a stove to a caveman — that was probably how Monsieur Clatoux felt all the time! How strange it must be, to be amongst such savages as herself! And yet he was infinitely patient and kind.

"First, let us save my life; next, we shall communicate with others of my kind. You told me of a mechanical device with spinning horses," he said.

"It may be this huge mound in the middle of the room," she said, tugging at the tarp. It was almost too much of an effort, and Monsieur himself was weakening by the minute, but presently the entire device was uncovered. It was in fact a species of merry-go-round. From an awning hung various metal bars, which were designed to jingle when touched.

There was a tall pillar in the middle, and around the pillar there were horses of various materials: stuffed cloth, metal, and wood. Each was attached to the central pillar by a spoke, and a small platform above the plane of the spokes bore a sort of giant crank, an oversized version of something one might see on a music-box. The horses were not equidistant from the central pillar; when the whole revolved, therefore, the velocity of the horses in the perimeter would exceed those nearer the centre, even though they were moving in tandem.

"You must place me on one of the horses," Monsieur said. "Thence, attach me to my communication device by way of these" … he indicated them… "wires. Just stick them into my head; my flesh is not really flesh, merely an illusion, so they will not pain me. And wheel the entire device to the platform at the center."

It was pitiful to watch Monsieur clamber onto the saddle of the nearest horse. He had to clutch it by its neck to steady himself.

"Now, listen carefully. First, you must turn the crank as far as it will go. Then, sit down on the velocipede's seat — I know it will be uncomfortable and may even arouse unwelcome sensations inside your unmentionables, but we have come too far for that kind of queasiness now. You will find the meteorite is situated deep inside the device, below the space between your legs, for this is no time to be riding sidesaddle! When I give the signal, you will start squeezing the onion onto the meteorite, and when I give a second signal, you will release the crank and begin pedalling as fast as you possibly can — in the opposite direction from the spin of this merry-go-round. If the contraption starts to lose speed, you must crank it some more! Do you understand?"

"So ... I am to perch precariously on the battered seat of this broken velocipede, turn, then release a crank with one hand whilst squeezing an onion under my petticoats with the other?" Arabella said, wondering what Mrs. Dorrit would think. Still, it was the last chance to save Monsieur and their entire family from ruin. She began cranking with a will. The device sighed and creaked, but did not seem to move.

"Do not fear," said Monsieur. "The contraption is storing up a supply of power which will be released as kinetic energy which will burst forth all at once, upon your next action."

She continued to turn the crank. It was hard work, more suited to a creature like Japheth than a gentlewoman like herself. Yet she hove to with a will. At each turn of the crank, it was harder to move.

"More!" said the Frenchman. "You must crank with every fibre of your being!"

"I can't any more!" The effort was overwhelming. She was soaked with sweat, and her thighs felt slick against the ill-padded seat of the velocipede. "I shall die, I'm sure!"

"Now!" said Monsieur. "Release!"

With her free hand she squeezed the onion with all her might, forcing the droplets with every effort of the will. She let go of the crank and began to pedal and all at once the entire merry-go-round started to lurch in the opposite direction, striking the metal bars in a slowly accelerating rendition of *Rule Britannia.*

She could sense a sizzling, buzzing sound in her nether regions. Glancing below, she could see that her petticoats appeared to be on fire. The flames were blue and cold, and seemed to be issuing from where the onion juice touched the meteorite. The fire was spreading. Her corset had become ice-cold. Her sweat was frosting over and turning blue.

"Heavens!" she cried. "Is this the desired result?"

She could hear Monsieur as he flailed and thrashed about on his horse. "The bacteria are fixing the dysprosium," he gasped.

The wire that connected his head to the device was stretching, thinning until it was almost invisible. "Monsieur!" Arabella exclaimed. "It will surely snap!"

"No," said Monsieur. "This wire is even more ductile than gold. Quick, Miss Dorrit! Another crank!"

She cranked, squeezed and pedalled with abandon. Monsieur heaved, was thrown about, and ... seemed to be liquefying before her very eyes! "You are melting into the very aether!" she cried. "I *must* stop pedalling, else you shall perish!"

She heard Monsieur's voice ... but it was not coming from the horse he sat on. Rather, it seemed to echo inside her skull. *You ... must ... continue ... metamorphosis ... essential to the operation ...*

The blue flames that had spread up from her thighs seemed to engulf her entire form. Yet she continued to pedal, crank, and squeeze. Monsieur was now a pool of liquid, and starting to evaporate, turning into a blue mist that spread, moving against the wind-current of the churning merry-go-round. *Rule Britannia* was louder now, the bells being joined by an invisible orchestra of strings, wind, and brass, which seemed to be emanating from other automata at the perimeter of the chamber. Mechanicals birds swarmed the air.

The blue mist began to infiltrate her nostrils. She pedalled with increasing celerity. Something in the fumes … but of course, they partook of the essence of Monsieur … they *were* Monsieur, indeed! Monsieur was invading her very flesh. It was a feeling even more intimate than when His Lordship the Earl had … she blushed even as the gaseous Monsieur began filtering through the porous fabric of her petticoats.

"Heavens, Monsieur!" she exclaimed. "Should you really be making love to me while the world goes up in blue flames?"

"Of course, my dear Miss Arabella," came the inner voice. "It is lovemaking that is at the heart of all being — the dance of neutrons and neurons, the symphony of nerves and superstrings, the paradox of the expanding universe and the shrinking event horizon — all these are conflated in the cosmic choreography of creation!"

Unnameable feelings stirred in Arabella. It was not lust. It was nothing shameful. Rather, it was a kind of exaltation. The cold blue flames consumed her utterly. She gave in to the torrential emotions. These were emotions so overwhelming they could not be possibly be human, let alone English.

At length, with the merry-go-round spinning so fast that it must needs pull free of the central pillar, she found herself volleying into the night sky, writhing in the embrace of the flames. And she too felt herself turning first to fluid then to crimson mist which intermingled with Monsieur's to form a pulsating purple cloud. She screamed again and again, not in pain but in perilous passion, though the screams came not from her throat but her entire being.

Suddenly, it was as though the sky opened up. Thousands upon thousands of voices sang to her.   They were angels — divine beings from another world — though she also knew they were just all Frenchman like Monsieur Clatoux. She was in full communion with races and species heretofore unimagined. It was an absolute ecstasy. She wondered whether even her uncle, in his communion with the Divine, had ever encountered so sublime an epiphany.

And then it was over.

Miss Arabella, returned to her sublunary form, landed on the floor in a heap, entwined with Monsieur.

But this was not the suave, well-muscled blue man she knew so well. Monsieur had turned into something resembling a two-headed octopus, with a frightening assemblage of claws, jaws, and maws. She screamed and ran to the wall, only to realize there was no wall. The entire Mechanical Exhibition was a pile of smoking rubble, and they were surrounded by some of London's seamier back alleys, being peered at by a motley assortment of urchins, beggars, and women of the night.

Monsieur was still blue. Apart from that, there was nothing familiar about him at all, and when he spoke, it was a metallic clattering combined with an eerie whine.

"Do not be afraid," he said. "I have been much weakened, and am currently unable to retain my true shape. However, I shall soon be back to normal — at least, as your kind perceives normal."

"What has happened?"

"Happened? Why, my dear Miss Arabella, the communication has been a success! The energy released by the contrary motion of velocipede and merry-go-round, magnified a trillionfold by the dysprosium-fixing action of the bacteria when awakened by the onion juice catalyst, has allowed a temporary spacetime anomaly to exist wherein it was possible for me to send a superluminal communication to my, ah, fellow Frenchmen."

"So we are saved?"

"They will arrive within days. Meanwhile, we must bring to a conclusion the marital affairs of the entire Dorrit family, set up Mr. Bumbry in an episcopal sinecure, and stage the grandest ball ever seen in Little Chiswick."

"But Monsieur … you're an octopus."

"Pray give me a moment or two, Miss Arabella. I aim to moult ere we depart."

30

Lord Chuzzlewit

The two-headed blue octopus shed its skin and the old Monsieur stepped out. He was if anything even more magnificent than the first day Arabella had met him. His blue skin glistened in the gaslight. He knelt down to pick up the flayed skin and proceeded to eat it, nibbling away from tentacle to crown until there was nothing left. As he consumed his own skin, clothing began to form on his naked body. He had a linen shirt, a cutaway coat, a purple cravat, and dark grey breeches coupled with white stockings, and each article of clothing appeared to have been delivered spanking-new from the tailor within the hour.

He was, indeed, dressed for the ball itself, although the ball could not transpire immediately. Since the clothes were not actual clothes, but merely simulacra that held their shape through Monsieur's exercise of his scientific powers, Arabella reflected that to touch, say, a frill on the front of his chemise thus, was to touch the naked flesh it-self — a miracle not unlike the Roman Catholics' benight-ed view of transubstantiation — except that she knew it not to be magic, but science!

And what a thrill, not only to have touched his flesh in the past hour, but actually to have been subsumed into his very essence in the form of a mist!

Ignoring the riff-raff in the London street, and no longer having to wheel the velocipede-powered-telephone, Arabella and Monsieur made their way easily to the ship and were whisked off to the orchard behind the vicarage.

It was nearly dawn, and the Dorrits were breakfasting al fresco, *en famille.*

Japheth and Pauline immediately set two more places and Mrs. O'Keefe emerged with a splendid platter of kip-pers.

"We're home," Arabella announced, "and we're ready for the final spectacle."

Mrs. Dorrit, her daughters finally back with her, and with a wedding to plan, had reason to feel contented. Dur-ing Anna's disappearance, and Arabella's rescue mission, she had been compiling a guest list for what was going to be the most glittering ball the ton had ever seen.

"Oh, Mother," Arabella was saying. "It is so wonderful to see you happy at last."

"I should be even happier," Mrs. Dorrit said, "if Anna, too, were settled."

Miss Anna sighed. "And were *I* to be settled, Mama, would not *you* become lonely? And might *you* not need companionship? It has been so long since Papa's passing, and you have always taught us that a man should be the centre of our world."

Arabella laughed. "You may have *taught* us that," she said, "But we all know that you run rings round Mr. Bumbry."

"Indeed," Mrs. Dorrit said, glad that one daughter, at least, understood the true workings of the world.

Mr. Bumbry, still forlorn after the revelations of his secret vices, did not speak much. He sat there, marking up guest lists and grimly sipping his tea.

Anna said, "I don't need to be courted, Mother. I'm perfectly happy to play the pianoforte. Perhaps I should like to be come a professional performer!"

Mr. Bumbry interposed, "My dear, you know you can't be on a stage. We're respectable people."

"Respectable!" said Anna. "Really, Uncle."

Mrs. Dorrit said, "Brother, I don't think your views on respectability can be taken seriously at this juncture."

"But I shall soon be a bishop, and have my own cathedral."

"Well, naturally, your words will have more weight then," she said, wondering whether her brother even realized the irony in that sentiment. Then she added, "If my daughter wishes to be a pianist … or even to sing in something so scandalous as … an *Italian opera,* I should not say a word. If there's anything I've learnt from the Frenchman's sojourn chez nous, it is that a woman may think freely, have a mind of her own, and might have a better eye for the right man than her parents might think. After all, I should never have guessed that our own Arabella was destined to be a Countess! Why should not Anna be whatever she wishes to be? With Arabella spoken for, our family's fate is by no means unenviable. Even if Anna were not properly matched, the Dorrit's would still reign unchallenged over the entire ton."

"She may not remain unmatched long," Mr. Bumbry muttered, for a barouche was drawing near — the barouche that Mrs. Dorrit had had occasion to borrow in the past.

"Good Heavens!" said Mrs. Dorrit, when Japheth went to help its occupant alight. "Lord Chuzzlewit!"

Japheth announced: "Mr Bumbry, Mrs. and the Misses Dorrit, Monsieur Clatoux: The Rt. Honourable Alasdaire Fenton-Bumbry, Lord Chuzzlewit."

"No need to announce me, my good man! Good morning, Cousin," said His Lordship, and Mrs. Dorrit was keenly aware that His Lordship rarely deigned to address her as *cousin*. Was it simply that the Dorrits would soon be higher than he on the Order of Precedence?

"Why, my Lord," she said.

"Just call me Alasdaire," Lord Chuzzlewit said.

"I wouldn't presume," said Mrs. Dorrit.

"But you shall presume," said His Lordship. "You shall very much presume, my dear cousin. For I come in order to request, formally, the privilege of calling on Miss Anna."

Arabella said, "Mother dear, I believe that there is something Monsieur and I must do at Flanders House. Perhaps it may be expedient for my Uncle, too, to be about his business; surely he has a sermon to write, or what have you. Meanwhile, you should remain as chaperone, for you know that we Dorrit women are prone to compromising situations."

Mrs. Dorrit watched as her brother, the servants, and her other daughter and the Frenchman all vanished, rather quickly, into thin air.

"May I?" said Lord Chuzzlewit, who was probably not expecting the others to disappear with such alacrity.

Mrs. Dorrit invited His Lordship to sit at the table, and began to butter him a piece of toast, whilst Anna sat across from him, attempting to look demure.

"I know I am forward," said His Lordship, "but I confess that I did have the pleasure of accidentally encountering Miss Anna before. I believe she had lost her way, and was looking for the *petite chambre*. We did admire a painting together."

"The *Rape of Ganymede*," Anna said. "Uncle would have loved it, I sure, for it showed the mighty Jove with a somewhat more rampant manhood than one has come to expect in an artwork of the Renaissance."

"Luckily," said Lord Chuzzlewit, "a large shaft of chiaroscuro covered the actual, ah, equipment."

"Indeed! — leaving more to the imagination than one might think humanly possible."

"Well, the Olympians are Gods, after all," said His Lordship.

The conversation is going in a rather provocative direction, thought Mrs. Dorrit. *Surely my daughter hasn't already ...* Perhaps there were darker reasons to pursue her daughter's hand. She cleared her throat very loudly, and said in her sweetest, most threatening voice, "You know, I've always been curious about the real worth of Your Lordship's estate."

"What, you mean in terms of money?" he said, nonplussed.

"Pounds per annum," she said. "I believe you understand what we mean."

31

Pavilion of Wonders

The sight of Flanders House stirred in Miss Arabella's soul a welter of contradictory emotions.

From her accidental first encounter with the Earl to the very purposeful encounters she had had most recently, Arabella had been on a terrifying, enthralling journey. Now, unchaperoned save by a man to whom she had once made love in the form of a shower of blue mist, she would set eyes on him again.

The butler admitted them, and informed them that the Rt. Honourable Tobias David Chrysostom George Mary Durham-St. Aubin-Borgnis, Ninth Earl of Little Chiswick and Viscount Blueborough, was breakfasting, but had given standing instructions than Miss Arabella be admitted into his presence at any hour of the day or night, no matter the rules of propriety.

In a private dining room at Flanders House, seated at one end of an almost interminable table, the Earl sat. He was flanked by an elderly, distinguished woman in black on his left, and a Catholic priest on his right.

"So this is she," said the woman, "who has plunged my home into hideous heresy!"

Arabella realized immediately that this must be the Dowager Countess.

"Good morning, dearest Arabella," said the Earl. "My mother, as you can see, has decided to take up residence in Flanders House after a period of self-imposed exile in our estates in Avignon. Mother dear, this is Miss Dorrit, and the Frenchman Monsieur Clatoux, whom Tante Charlotte has recently received at court."

"*Enchantée,*" said the Countess frostily.

"*Mit vorzüglicher Hochachtung,*" said Monsieur, using the wrong phrase in the wrong language.

"And this," said the Earl, indicating the padre who sat across from his mother, "is my mother's confessor, Father Impedimento."

"I've summoned him here," said the Dowager, "to ensure that this Anglican travesty that is about to occur does not have the unintended consequence of making our Toby perforce *live in sin.*"

"We didn't quite get to that stage, mother. I *had* summoned a priest already, as you know, but we were interrupted by a most peculiar family crisis which prompted Arabella to make a positively *mythical* journey to Russia."

"I might add, within the entrails a whale," said Arabella.

"Stuff and nonsense," said the Dowager Countess.

"Nevertheless," said Father Impedimento, "it appears I am to serve in the role of Friar Lawrence to this star-crossed couple."

"Get on with it," said the Dowager Countess.

"Are there rings?" said the priest.

The Earl reached into a pocket and produced a golden ring topped with a monstrous carbuncle, perhaps worth as much as the entire vicarage. "I had another, a more tasteful one," he sighed, "but this one will have to do. And it seems that Mother and Monsieur may serve as witnesses."

"It's such a shame," said the Dowager Countess, "that we must perform the true marriage ceremony in this tawdry manner, against this vista of half-eaten kippers … and that the mockery of a Protestant solemnization will occur with pomp and ceremony, in an actual cathedral, presided over by a so-called bishop!"

"Mother!" said the Earl. "You speak as though Thomas Cromwell were about to burn you at the stake."

"He burned your great-great-great-grandfather," said the Dowager Countess.

"This is the nineteenth century," said His Lordship. "We're not barbarians."

"Your Ladyship," said Monsieur.

"Stop interrupting our family conversation," said the Dowager Countess. "In fact — begone!"

"I merely wish to point out, Your Ladyship," he said, "that there is no need for a tawdry ceremony over an uncleared breakfast table. For if all of you would but step through the back door into the grounds behind this house…."

Only now did Arabella comprehend the vastness of Monsieur Clatoux's power. For where there had been back gardens, a huge structure was erecting itself. It was as massive as any royal palace, and liberally accented with gold. There were towering columns with fanciful capitals, with a roof like a Greek temple, supported by a sculpted frieze representing scenes from mythologies Greek, Roman, and Egyptian, and others not even human, blue creatures in octopus-like form, drifting through alien landscapes. Leading up to the huge marble façade was a walkway lined with statues of fantastical creatures, from dragons and unicorns to grotesque creatures that perhaps belonged to the world of the blue octopodes.

"Behold, Miss Arabella, Your Lordship," said Monsieur. "I offer this to you as a small wedding gift. For I have made contact with the others of my race now, and I have replenished my energy sources for a brief span."

"But how could such thing have been erected whilst we were having breakfast?" said the Dowager Countess. "For this monument was not there at dawn."

"It is a process known as transmutive replication," said the Frenchman. "A tremendous amount of energy is required, so I shall no longer be able to produce any more lavish gifts until I return to my world. But I wished to give you this, as a small token of my esteem, for saving my life."

"Amazing!" said the Earl. "This is the proof that our religious doctrine of transubstantiation has a basis in science — and not the hocus-pocus imputed by the protestants."

"There must be some trick," said the Countess. "This cannot be real."

"Indeed it is not," said the Frenchman. "For at exactly midnight, on the evening of the ball, the entire Pavilion of Wonders will resolve back into its constituent elements, the molecules that form the gardens of your estate; all will be back to normal."

They entered the edifice. It was overwhelming. Three times life-size, a painting of Arabella gazing adoringly into the eyes of the Earl depended from the far wall. A luxurious Persian carpet covered the entire floor, of the type that would have taken years for weavers of the Orient to create.

"Well, this is all very well," said the Dowager Countess with grudging admiration, "but splendid as it is, we can't have the wedding here; it's not a proper church, for it has no genuine relic. But I would be willing to consider moving from the breakfast room to the chapel of the estate."

"But if the servants chance to stumble on the ceremony in progress, they might gossip," said Arabella, "and the scandal of a popish wedding might lessen the impact of His Lordship's putative conversion to the Protestant faith."

"I have thought of that," said Monsieur, taking a small phial out of his inner pocket. "I have taken the liberty of synthesizing a fragment of the True Cross just for the occasion."

He handed it to the astonished priest.

"Heavens!" said Father Impedimento. "But you've no proof!"

"Nonsense, Father," said the Dowager resolutely. "You've no proof of any *other* fragment of the True Cross either. Very well then, get on with it."

"Very well!" said the priest. Placing the relic on the nearest table, kissing it reverently, he turned to the Earl. "Tobias Davidus Chrysostomus Georgius," he said. "vis accipere Arabellam hic praesentatem in tuam legitimam uxorem juxta ritum sanctae matris Ecclesiae?"

His Lordship responded, "I haven't the foggiest notion what that means, so I think I'll just say 'Yes.' And so, I am sure, does Miss Arabella."

So saying, he took the carbuncle and slid it on to Arabella's finger, and kissed her passionately, not waiting for the rest of the ceremony. Confused, Father Impedimento made the sign of the cross.

"So, Monsieur," His Lordship continued, "Did you happen to provide a nuptial chamber somewhere in all this foreign architecture?"

"To the left of the painting, there's an arras, and a secret passageway."

"Very well then. We shall not delay the rapture further. Come, my dearest! Let me show you a few tricks I learnt in America!"

The Earl lifted Arabella in his arms and strode towards the arras.

32

Mr. Field's Last Nocturne

Let us draw the curtain gently over the first real intimacies between the Earl and his new-minted Countess.

Nay, rather, let us return to the vicarage, where Mrs. Dorrit is on the cusp of victory over the entire gossip-rife population of the ton; where Mr. Bumbry, rather than being consigned to universal opprobrium, is about to assume a bishopric; and where Lord Chuzzlewit, admittedly a much lower figure in the aristocratic hierarchy than the Earl of Little Chiswick, is even now paying court to Miss Anna, whom the world once considered homely, talentless and mealy-mouthed.

Let us not forget Mr Field, either. He was after all a distinguished visitor, the most famed practitioner of the pianoforte in all of England. He couldn't very well be kept waiting whilst a family negotiated matches.

He had been standing a little diffidently in the background, but when Monsieur and Arabella departed, he inquired as to whether the cottage might have an instrument available.

"Negotiate whatever marriages you wish," he said. "As long as I may play my music, and there is an adequate supply of good English tea, you may forget about my existence until you have finished your discussions."

Mrs. O'Keefe took over the care of Mr. Field, sending Pauline off to brew the tea and retiring to the kitchen to concoct some sweetmeats.

"I shall compose a new nocturne," he informed them.

"In our very home?" Anna exclaimed. "Why, it is an enviable honour indeed!"

"When I have finished my composition," said Mr. Field, "I'll give a shout!"

"And we'll all consume one of Mrs. O'Keefe's famous eel pies," said Mrs. Dorrit.

Miss Anna Dorrit had undergone quite a transformation since her sojourn in the Tsar's court. Her accomplishments on the pianoforte no longer needed to be shored up by Monsieur's magic. She had found herself able to unlock passions buried deep within herself. And now, sitting in the orchard over tea, with phrases from Mr. Field's pregnant imagination flying in through the open window of the parlour, Miss Anna felt quite liberated from the conventions with which she had fettered herself in the past.

Her mother had inquired about how many "pounds per annum" accrued to His Lordship's estate. She dismissed her mother's bargaining and boldly dived into the conversation herself.

"Oh, Mother!" she said. "Let us not be tawdry. As the in-laws of an Earl, we shall lack for nothing. Let me be frank, my Lord," she continued. "My mother is desirous of seeing me settled, but I don't give a tinker's dam about it."

"Heavens!" said Mrs. Dorrit.

"I come to you with no dowry, or virtually none," she said. "Why, even this vicarage I live in is available to me only because of your good will."

"This is hardly the time to speak of the disadvantages of such a match," said her mother. "Why don't you leave the room and I and Mr. Bumbry, as your guardians, shall make the arrangements befitting to our position."

"With all due respect, Mother," said Anna, "and appropriately to you, my dear uncle, bugger off."

Lord Chuzzlewit began to laugh uproariously at this. Indeed, his guffaws brought Mrs. O'Keefe running out, rolling pin in hand.

"My dear Mrs. Dorrit," said His Lordship, "with such a fiery temperament, I should marry her a thousand times over! She shall be a holy terror in the household, and she will dominate those meekly squawking gossips of the ton … perhaps even shock them to silence!"

"I do not, of course, love you, Your Lordship," said Miss Anna.

"Rubbish!" her mother said. "What on Earth does that have to do with marriage?"

"Why, nothing, my dear cousin," said Lord Chuzzlewit. "The first Lady Chuzzlewit knew about as much about love as a blancmange. Yet she *did* profess to love me. I care not for such protestations."

"What you *do* care about," said Miss Anna, "is my capacity to produce the next Lord Chuzzlewit. You're not that young, and your first wife seems not to have produced any offspring. You've cleverly calculated that I'm the likeliest prospect out of a very bad batch, Your Lordship."

"Won't you call me Alasdaire, my dear?"

"I too have made a number of extremely practical calculations. Your finances are adequate and far less likely to be in a mess than the Earl's. You're eminently solid. I thought I was solid, as well, nay, perfectly grounded, but now it seems I am about to take flight. I need someone like you betimes, to keep me attached to the earth."

"I see no reason to wait, in that case," said Lord Chuzzlewit.

"I agree," said Anna. "If I wait another day, I shall be an old maid."

Bowing deeply to Mrs. Dorrit, The Right Honourable Alasdaire Fenton-Bumbry, Lord Chuzzlewit, said, "Let us eschew the traditional engagement, then, and have a double wedding on the morrow."

Mr. Bumbry said, "Good Heavens! I shall have to have a double homily."

"You shall be brief, brother," said Mrs. Dorrit, trying without much success to suppress her glee.

"But you, dearest Mama," said Miss Anna. "Now that your daughters are about to be settled, will *you* not marry?"

Mrs. Dorrit laughed. 'What!" she said. "I, marry?"

At that very moment, an exquisite music came floating down from the window. It was Mr. Field's nocturne, no longer in fragments, but whole. It was in equally parts mournful and joyful. It soared; it swooped; its shifting harmonies swept through the air like a wind.

"What indeed! I, marry?" Mrs. Dorrit said again.

And yet … Mr. Field's last nocturne seemed to sing of a world in which all things were possible.

If there was anything Mrs. Dorrit had learnt from the coming of the Frenchman from the stars, it was to be able to see her world for the comedy it was, and the little plaints and peccadilloes so harped on by the local gossips to be mere ripples in a cosmic pond.

The advent up the aisle of a second happy couple was a little unexpected by most of the ton, but Miss Anna's wedding dress occasioned as many gasps as Arabella's. Indeed, Monsieur had created it — and Miss Arabella's costume as well — the previous night, using the last few droplets left to him. "If you need any more of this so-called magic," he had told the three women, "you shall have to wait for me to recharge fully in the mother ship," a sentiment as mysterious as it was disappointing.

As befit the lower level of nobility to which Lord Chuzzlewit belonged, Miss Anna's was a lesser spectacle, but appeared equally costly. She and her beau came up the aisle hard on the heels of the Earl and Countess, so they arrived at the altar just as the traditional osculation was ending.

Mrs. Dorrit could hardly restrain her tears. "Why, Monsieur," she said to the blue-faced Frenchman who shared her pew, "Years of Machiavellian machinations availed me naught; yet in a single season you have made all my dreams come true!"

"Does not one dream remain, my dear Mrs. Dorrit?" said Monsieur Clatoux. "Or dare I call you … Emma?"

Mrs. Dorrit blushed. To her own amazement, she realized that the Frenchman had been holding her hand. "Why, monsieur! The ton will talk!"

"Tonight I depart for the furthest reaches of the galaxy," he said. "Let them talk!"

"Gossip won't touch you all the way up there, in France," said Mrs. Dorrit. "But here in England ..."

"Unless ..." Monsieur Clatoux said, his eyes twinkling.

... and then came the Ball to End All Balls.

The whole of the foyer of Flanders House served merely a receiving area for the guests, to leave their cloaks, swords, and of course, wedding gifts. It seemed that the entire contents of the Garden of Eden had been laid within this anteroom. The fragrances overwhelmed the nostrils.

To reach the ball, one went in through the front, deposited one's gifts and accoutrements, and then went out through the back and into the gardens, where Monsieur's phantasmagorical pavilion rose, taller than a cathedral, more luminous than a Greek temple in the moonlight. Guests were gaping in wonderment, pointing out the statues, friezes and columns, and having footmen proffering flutes of the finest champagne before they even set foot inside.

Mrs. Dorrit stood at the façade of the pavilion, greeting the guests. The pachydermic Mrs. Sanditon! The Farthingale brothers, hunting new conquests! The seductive Miss Talliaferro! Mrs. Gotham-Clarke, shepherding her daughters and warding off the wolves with a fold of her pelisse!

"Hurry," Mrs. Dorrit said to the latter, "before Edna, Edwina and and Evangeline become undesirables at twenty, and old maids at twenty-two!"

"You're certainly enjoying this," said the Dowager Countess, who, while eschewing the nuptials, would not have missed the ball for all the world.

"Aren't you, Your Ladyship?" said Mrs. Dorrit, smiling sweetly. "These are the very people who call you a harridan, a harpy, and worst, a Hell-bound papist behind your back."

"Well, I've certainly been all those things," said the Dowager Countess, laughing. "And I shan't change. But since I can't very well do battle with my wayward son's designs — and he is the actual Earl, while I am merely a vestige of the previous regime — I suppose I shall simply grin and bear it."

"Most gracious, Your Ladyship," said Mrs. Dorrit.

The convoy from the church was now arriving. The Earl and his new Countess did not enter through the lobby, but came round the side of the building, in order to display to all a sumptuous carriage that had been lent by Their Majesties themselves. Following closely after were Lord and Lady Chuzzlewit, this time, for once, riding in the best instead of the second-best barouche. On foot, or stepping through the foyer of the main hall into the gardens, were the other celebrants, including Monsieur, the Rt. Reverend Bumbry, Deacon Japheth, and so on.

From behind the façade, there came the sound of a *symphonical* orchestra tuning; this was the most accomplished such orchestra in all England, including some geriatric members who had played in Mr. Haydn's first tour of London, and a violinist who had actually played with Mr. Handel as a young boy. They were striking up one of the newfangled German Waltzes, a dance style so sensational the partners actually touched with shocking familiarity. Mrs. Dorrit did not care. Her sense of propriety was no longer offended by such things. It was the happiest day of her life.

She smiled as Anna and Lord Chuzzlewit swept into the chamber and smiled even more to hear the applause from within the pavilion.

Countess Arabella raced up the steps alone, leaving the Earl waiting at the door of the carriage. She appeared in some distress.

"Arabella," said Mrs. Dorrit. "Are you quite all right?"

The newly-minted Countess shook her arm abruptly. "Mother!" she whispered urgently. "Come with me to the *petite chambre!* I have a *petit problème!*"

Quickly making her excuses, Mrs. Dorrit crossed the walkway with her daughter in tow. "Let us not seem too conspicuous," she said softly. "I am sure it's just the strain of this day." She nodded to the Earl and motioned for him to wait for a moment.

Arabella, Countess of Chiswick led her mother through the secret passage that led to the chamber. When they reached the room, she flung herself at the chamberpot, which was concealed beneath a velvet seat, and began regurgitating, loudly and abundantly.

"Mother," she said, "I've been vomiting since morning."

"My dear," said Mrs. Dorrit, "I'm sure you're quite aware of what that means, and I am not surprised, seeing how flagrantly you've behaved with His Lordship. But you're married now. How can a week or so matter?"

"That is not my fear, Mother! The problem is ... my vomitus is a most unsubtle shade of blue!"

"There, there, my dear. Monsieur Clatoux will devise a solution, I am sure —"

"Monsieur is returning to the stars, Mama, and I shall presently give birth to a two-headed cerulean octopus!"

At that moment, they heard a dramatic flourish of trumpets from the lawn.

"Their Majesties!" said Mrs. Dorrit. "You'd better hurry up and finish vomiting."

34

A Dilemma in Blue

Mrs. Dorrit emerged a few moments later with her daughter the Countess. They found the Earl still waiting at the carriage. An even more resplendent carriage, bearing Their Majesties, had already arrived in front of the pavilion, and within, the orchestra had launched into the drumroll that presaged the performance of *God Save the King*.

Quickly, Anna and Lord Chuzzlewit came to stand beside them. Mrs. Dorrit, the proud mother, would walk just behind the royal couple and the newlyweds; to her great relief, she found Monsieur approaching.

"I shall be your escort," Monsieur said, "for, having been knighted by His Majesty, I may be entitled to a certain precedence."

Mrs. Dorrit whispered, "My daughter has made known to me a matter of the gravest consequence."

"Ah! She has told you how we managed to make contact with the others of my kind."

"And the contact between the two of you?" said Mrs. Dorrit, barely able to contain her discomfiture.

The Frenchman laughed. "It is of little consequence."

So saying, he placed her arm across her shoulders, and they proceeded into the pavilion to the strains of the National Anthem.

The ball beggared description. Nothing like it was ever seen before, nor will ever be seen again in Little Chiswick. The ostentatious display of the latest styles! The delicate minuets, careful quadrilles, wild waltzes! Lady Chuzzlewit's turn on the pianoforte, during the course of which a whirlwind actually sprang up from the keys and sprinkled gold dust on the faces of the guests!

She was beyond contentment. True, she was not *in* love with her suddenly acquired husband, but she found him most tolerable; she was a little wary of the coming rites of the bedchamber, but she was vaguely aware that something both rapturous and painful would happen later.

That was, of course, the story of her life. It was Arabella who had been blessed with all the charm, and most of the accomplishments. She had compensated for her being found wanting by society by exhibiting a willfully unsavoury series of traits, such as playing the pianoforte badly, and uttering unseemly vulgarities at inappropriate moments.

The Frenchman had seemed to open up her abilities by some sort of magical power, but her sojourn in Russia, and her time with Mr. Field, had come to reveal to her that her inner self was as beautiful as her sister's, nay, as truthful, too.

Arabella, Countess of Little Chiswick and Viscountess Blueborough, was in confusion after her cerulean regurgitation. Should she tell David? Should she keep it from him, and hope that Monsieur would intervene, in some deus ex machina-like way, to extricate her from this predicament? But Monsieur was leaving virtually on the instant. And he himself had told her he was practically depleted of all energy. And why would he want to do something that might jeopardize his own offspring?

Unless it were *not* offspring. Hadn't the Frenchman told her that his race had *seven* genders, all of which were required to participate in a successful act of reproduction? But in the night of purple mist, she had not recalled the presence of five *more* Frenchmen. Surely she would have remembered that.

She went to find David.

The Earl was deep in conversation with Their Majesties, who were enthroned together. It took some time for Arabella to get through to the twin thrones, for every few seconds someone stopped to proffer a word of congratulation. She tried her best to appear gracious to every guest.

She curtsied before the thrones; Her Majesty beckoned with a crooked finger.

"Schätzchen!" the Queen murmured.

"Your Majesty," Arabella replied, curtsying even lower, flattered to be apostrophized with so teutonic an endearment; Her Majesty truly must view her as family. How would she react, then, to a grand-nephew with blue skin? The infamy! It was not to be borne. By definition, royals had fair skin, for of the human race they were the closest to the purity of godhead.

"Your Lordship," she said to her husband, for she was not yet entirely used to addressing him informally, and the Earl made his excuses.

"Something has occurred," she whispered to him, as the orchestra struck up another quadrille, "of the utmost urgency. Indeed, you may wish to put me aside when I tell you."

"Heavens!" said the Earl. "I pray you, let us take the air."

He took her by the hand and they went through the hidden curtain, behind where the altar had stood when Father Impedimento performed the secret, Catholic ceremony.

Aside from the secret bedchamber where they had celebrated the nuptial union, there was also a stairway that led directly to the grounds. This part of the estate was rarely frequented, as there were many convoluted pathways in the back gardens.

"Now," said the Earl, "you are being silly. Perhaps you're finally overcome by the prospect of your coming rank in society."

"Hardly," said Arabella. "For I care not a fig for rank, unless it allows me to attend meetings of the Royal Society despite my sex."

"Is *that* all?" said the Earl. "I'll have the House of Lords create a special dispensation for you!"

"I'm afraid that … this evening … after the church service … I was feeling faint. This evening, I fell prey to morning sickness!"

"I fail to understand how you can have morning sickness in the evening," said the Earl. "You *are* being silly."

"Nay, my Lord, 'morning sickness' is just a newfangled term for *hyperemesis gravidarum.*"

"My dearest," said the Earl, "There's no need to impress me with your learning. I'm only an Earl, you know."

"I am … I'm afraid that I might be …" she could not bring herself to say it in her mother tongue "… *je suis enceinte,*" she managed at last.

"Try German," said the Earl.

"*Schwanger,*" she managed.

"Why," he said, "that is simply splendid! But how could you know so soon? Back in Virginia, it might weeks before one of my slaves would tell me."

"Slaves?" said Arabella. "They still have them there? But it was just abolished, in 1807."

"My dear Countess," said the Earl, "America is a primitive land. I know that it has driven Uncle George mad, but it is truly a continent well lost."

"Yet you did not give up your tobacco farm."

"I could not," he said. "Until my own mismanagement took it from me. I was, alas, more interested in the women than the earth."

"You have … bastards?" said Arabella.

"Well, hardly. They were but chattel, whereas you … you have intellect, and character, and immense fortitude.

You shall be my bulwark, my foundation, my flying buttress."

"And if my own child were the offspring of another?"

"That were quite impossible, my dear. Why, you bled like a doe *dans la chasse*. The Blessed Virgin could not have been more *intacta*, if you know what I mean."

"Oh, so you *do* understand Latin."

"None too well, dearest," he said. "But I have owned a plantation. I have managed farms. I know the uncomfortable reality about the mating of animals, and I assure you, Arabella, those of humans are no less bestial, though we might fancify them with fine poetry and music."

"So you are saying I am *not…*"

He laughed. "Of course not," he said. "At the moment I possessed you, you were as pure a bluestocking as could possibly be encountered."

Somehow, Arabella was not comforted. There were things in the universe, she knew, that could not be explained by the couplings of farm animals. She had to find Monsieur Clatoux. Only Monsieur could explain. He had the wisdom of other worlds. He was the one who had come from beyond.

"Listen!" said the Earl.

She started to protest, but he stopped her with a kiss.

She could hear music coming from the pavilion. The sound of the orchestra, beginning a lilting waltz. It was magical. Even from this distance, it brightened the darkness, pulled moonlight from behind a cloud, caused the stars to shine.

"Dance with me," he said.

"A waltz?" she said. "Alone? Is that … proper?"

"With you, my dear, all things shall be proper."

Upon the next kiss, thoughts of blue vomitus dissipated; she lived for the moment, confident that all would be made well.

35

The Passion of Mrs. Dorrit

At length, Mr. Field himself took the stage. For the first time that evening, there was absolute quiet.

Mr. Field was the greatest pianist and composer of the age, and he knew it well.   Szopinski was an impudent whippersnapper, a flash in the pan; Clementi's racing thirds were yesterday's excitement. There was no event as important to every young woman desirous of improving her accomplishments as the introduction of one of Mr. Field's nocturnes, and the double wedding was indubitably elevated to an event of world significance because of it. If not the *entire* world, at least the environs of Little Chiswick.

The nocturne began with a single note, high, repeated irregularly, like the chirping of a lone bird in the night; the note quickened, became a trill, as though the night-bird were spreading its wings and swooping from branch to branch in a moonlight forest.

Lady Chuzzlewit was entirely entranced, as was her new husband.

"I shall obtain this manuscript from Mr. Field," she whispered to His Lordship. "I shall copy it myself, and I shall make a point of learning it by rote, and playing it at our very first soirée. Our friends will be stunned."

"You may not have time for accomplishments, my dear," said Lord Chuzzlewit, "for you shall soon be creating masterpieces of your own. I refer, of course, to a new heir."

"I hope any child of mine will learn to love music," Anna said.

"He shall love anything that you love," Chuzzlewit said, "as I already do."

How contented she felt!

Now Mr. Field added a second melodic strand to the trilling solo line. It meandered under the higher melisma, adding a touch of melancholy. Then, with a series of staccato hopping chords, Mr. Field created the impression of frogs croaking after a thundershower. One by one, creatures of the night were being portrayed, in a contrapuntal symphony of owl, frog, nightingale, and thrush.

Then, surging upward out of the staccato bass line — there came a richly harmonized melody that was dripping with impossible yearning. Lady Chuzzlewit felt the pain of unrequited love.

"My dear Lord Chuzzlewit!" she cried out. "Perhaps we too, plain and ordinary and unimaginative as we are, may yet ascend to these Olympian heights."

"I hope so," said her husband, "for I do fear that the first Lady Chuzzlewit was something of a bore."

"I hope you will think you have found a better bargain on your second visit to the marriage market," said Anna.

"I daresay I have," said His Lordship.

Mr. Field's performance on the pianoforte was profoundly affecting. It occurred to Mrs. Dorrit that she had never actually heard a *man* play the pianoforte, although it was an accomplishment that was *de rigeur* for any woman of breeding. She had always been taught that men had loftier goals than the mere pursuit of accomplishments; but since Monsieur's advent, she had learnt a thing or two about her own sex, in particular that far from being the weaker, women truly ruled the world, whether it was Queen Charlotte in the palace, or the Tsarina bending the Russian nobility to her will simply by pointing to a samovar.

Mr. Field was that rare thing — a *professional* musician who had somehow managed to overcome the stigma of being a paid performer, and was viewed as a true artist. Of course, part of this came from the mystique of his having spent most of his time in the barbaric splendour of the Russian Emperor's court.

Mrs. Dorrit found herself deep in conversation with Monsieur. Not conversation, per se, for they were too respectful to speak too loudly over the nocturne.

They toasted her twin daughters and their great fortune, not to mention the change in status for Mrs. Dorrit and her wayward brother ... and the ex-slave, Japheth, as well.

At length, Mrs. Dorrit was emboldened to ask Monsieur: "Earlier, you called me Emma."

"Was it too forward of me?"

"Perhaps … if I were younger … it would be. Yet I did not find it unflattering. It is just that … I do not know *your* Christian name."

He laughed. "That, my dear Emma, is because I do not possess one."

"Not have one? Are you not a Christian?"

"That is one of the things about your culture that I have yet to comprehend. But my kind do not have two or three names; we have a different name for each entity with which we communicate. Since, at any one time, I have thousands of friends, enemies, and associates, I also have thousands of names. For instance, in my relationship with *you* —"

"There is a secret name that I must call you by?"

He motioned Mrs. Dorrit to draw closer. He whispered in her ear for several minutes.

"I don't think I could remember all that," she said.

"Nor could you very easily shriek it out in the throes of passion," said Monsieur, winking.

"Oh! Monsieur!"

"This reminds me that we do have some unfinished matter to discuss … the matter of your marriage."

"*Monsieur!* I am a widow, and your generosity has made me Queen of Little Chiswick. What more could I possibly need in life? I have achieved the acme of a decent woman's desires."

"And yet you know there's more," said Monsieur. "Perhaps even an *indecent* desire!"

Mr. Field's nocturne was crescendoing to a climax. Mrs. Dorrit could not believe he was doing it all with only ten fingers, for there were the swooping birds, the convoluted harmonies, and the surging love-melody that threaded its way through the music's lush textures.

And still, the entire hall was almost silent. Even the occasional clink of a champagne flute and whispered conversations seemed to form part of Mr. Field's composition, like the sound of shifting leaves, of twigs under a fox's footfall. Everything was part of the nocturne.

"Ah!" Mrs. Dorrit exclaimed, and followed this with a lengthy string of gibberish that just streamed out of her mouth, limpid and flowery.

"You remembered my name!" said Monsieur Clatoux.

She continued, spouting more polysyllables of an unknown tongue, her glossolalia ripped free from her lips like cosmic laughter. Her entire being was shuddering in ecstasy. So must the apostles have felt in that little room in Jerusalem on Pentecost, speaking in tongues for the first time! The rapture she was feeling bore little of religiosity, however. Nay, it leaned in the direction of sin rather than salvation. But she did not care. She was ineluctably moved by this Frenchman, in a way the late Mr. Dorrit never could have moved her when he took his pleasures!

"I believe I might possibly love you," she said, not caring that royalty was within earshot.

"You are more empathic than any of my other mates!" Monsieur whispered in a tone of incommensurate yearning.

But at this moment of apotheosis, Mrs. Dorrit's rêverie was interrupted by her daughter Arabella.

"Mother, I *must* speak to Monsieur!"

Arabella had abandoned the Earl and had charged through the throng of rapt listeners.

"My dear Countess," said Monsieur, "I was about to propose to your mother."

So focused was Arabella on her own dilemma, she appeared not to hear this momentous utterance at all. "I have to tell you that I have just been regurgitating … something *blue*," she said.

"You're with child! How wonderful!" said Monsieur. "You will be all right, I am sure. I should expect no more than about a thousand eggs."

"But — the affront to the mores of the ton —"

Mrs. Dorrit spoke up. "A greater affront, my dear, might be that the beautiful gown you are wearing appears to be dissolving into thin air."

"Heavens!" said Monsieur. "It must be almost midnight. When the hour strikes, I'm afraid you will be quite, quite naked."

36

L'Envoi

Countess Arabella looked down as the clock struck its final chime and realized that she was, indeed, completely naked, and that the eyes of the entire crowd were on her. That masterpiece of couture that Monsieur had conjured up had gone up in smoke. She screamed.

Where could she run?

The throng gave another shout and when Arabella whipped around she saw that her sister Anna was in the same condition, and also screaming.

"I told you," Monsieur said, "that my creations would expire at midnight."

Arabella said, "We are ruined, my sister and I!"

"Hardly," said Monsieur. He whipped off the covering from the nearest table, sending champagne and pork pies flurrying into the air, and threw it about the Countess's shoulders. Seizing another tablecloth, he flung it around the panicking Lady Anna. "There, there," he said. "It was but a momentary embarrassment."

Arabella drew the tablecloth tighter about her shoulders. To be sure, she was covered now. She was more worried about her mother's discomfiture than her own.

But worse things were to follow.

The entire pavilion was winking out.

Not just the pavilion.

The orchestra. The food. The champagne. It was all vanishing. Just as well, because the floor around the Countess, one moment a mess of splintered champagne flutes and bits of food, had transformed into lawn.

The guests were in tumult. Only Her Majesty sat in unperturbed splendour. His Majesty, on the other hand, had doffed his robes himself, in imitation of the Dorrit twins, and was running up and down, making strange bird-like noises.

So there they were. Hundreds of people, a Lady and a Countess wearing tablecloths, and a nude King, all chattering at the top of the lungs in midnight madness.

But Mr. Field, seemingly oblivious, was continuing to play. The crashing chords and thundering cadences gave way to a series of filigree passages in the upper octaves.

The night sky was suddenly full of light.

Hundreds of space-ships, just like the one in which Monsieur had first journeyed to the orchard by the vicarage, were bursting out of the darkness, each one a glittering globe of multicoloured light.

"Fireworks!" came the cry. The display was such a spectacle that people were forgetting that the walls, food, orchestra and waiters had vanished into thin air, or that an unclothed monarch was squawking amongst the hedges. That the ladies of the hour were now decorously swathed in Chantilly tablecloths was scarcely to be noticed either, since the lace the ladies wore now was almost as elaborate as their wedding gowns had been.

"My dear Mrs. Dorrit," Monsieur exclaimed. "Your daughter has done it! I have telephonically telecommunicated with our teleporting telepaths!"

"What on earth do you mean?"

"I am being rescued! And not a moment too soon, for I have used up the very final modica of my transmutational powers."

Gazing up to the Heavens, Mrs. Dorrit was awed at the spectacle of it. The vault of the sky, lit by a thousand starships, was like a cathedral, and the flying machines flickered like candles — why, if popery were this elevating to the eyes, she might have converted herself.

The starships hovered above, and now from each of them, standing on a shiny metallic disk, a blue-skinned individual emerged. Some were humanoid in appearance. Others resembled otters, lizards, and even plants. None of them wore any clothes. There was also an enormous blue octopus — somewhat matriarchal in aspect — who appeared to be the commander, for she was directing the others from the air by waving her tentacles.

The octopus remained in the air, but the other hovering disks landed in a circle around where the pavilion of wonders had stood, forming a sort of wall of extraordinary Frenchmen.

Slowly, the octopus began spinning.

The circle of Frenchmen started to tighten.

"Now!" said Monsieur Clatoux. "Mrs. Dorrit, you must decide!"

"Decide?"

"Cast off the bonds of Little Chiswick! All space and time await you! Come join my other spouses in a mighty lovemaking that will shake the galaxy! Visit a thousand worlds!"

"A thousand worlds? I haven't even been to France," said Mrs. Dorrit.

"Ah, the pristine purity of your vision!" said Monsieur Clatoux. "To meld with your perspective, to see with the innocent eyes of a primitive terrestrial female ... You are the final ingredient I have needed to make my life a perfect *ug'unnieth!*"

She could no longer resist.

Monsieur Clatoux had a certain scent that awoke in anyone who smelled it the taste of hidden desires. Imagine, then, this scent multiplied a hundredfold. Imagine the guests all breathing it in, letting this unearthly fragrance possess them utterly ... and abandoning their inhibitions, giving in to all manner of forbidden pleasures ... for stays and pantaloons and corsets were being loosened all around them ... it seemed that the denizens of the ton had abandoned everything that made them English.

"I shall go with you," Mrs. Dorrit whispered.

"But mother —" Arabella cried. "My problem!"

"Do not fear," said Monsieur Clatoux. "Your mother and I shall return in time for the egg-laying, and we shall dine on the larvae with gusto!"

So saying, he seized Mrs. Dorrit in his embrace. "I feel," she said, "as though my feet are not even touching the ground."

"They're not," said Monsieur, and Mrs. Dorrit saw that they were soaring at least two yards above the heads of the guests, who were uninhibitedly celebrating the rites of Bacchus and Venus, laughing, singing, and moaning, while Mr. Field, oblivious, continued to play.

They floated above the throng, which resembled more an orgy of ancient Roman debauchery than a civilized ball.

Mrs. Dorrit saw her daughter back in the arms of the Earl, and her other daughter coyly holding hands with Lord Chuzzlewit, and she could see that all was well in her world.

"Will Little Chiswick now become ... a sort of den of iniquity, then?" she said, as they skimmed over the Right Reverend Bumbry, who had doffed his vestments and was disporting recklessly with his deacon.

"Don't worry, my dear," said Monsieur. "We shall perform a global memory wipe ere we depart. They will wake up in their beds with nothing more than a headache, and vague recollection of having spent the most memorable evening of their lives ... could they but remember it!"

A staircase of light descended from the belly of the giant octopus, which she now understood was in reality a kind of mother ship in whose tentacles all the other vehicles would dock.

A beam of blue light shot out from the octopus's eye. Monsieur was enveloped in an angelic radiance. As they stood on the golden stair, Monsieur planted his lips firmly on Mrs. Dorrit's. The latter gazed down at her hands. Was it a trick of the moonlight?

"I'm turning blue," she gasped. "Am I suffocating?"

"Decidedly not," said Monsieur. "You are becoming! The blue comes from epidermal secretions that will allow you to survive in space by photosynthesizing starlight."

"I see," she said. Well, she supposed she would see once she got the hang of it.

"Wave farewell to Little Chiswick," said Monsieur.

They entered the belly of the octopus; within was a chamber that precisely resembled her bedroom back at the vicarage. "I thought you should have quarters that feel familiar," said Monsieur. "Look out of the window."

They were ascending.

She saw the whole of Flanders House now, including the corner of the grounds where the witches' sabbat of a ball was still proceeding in earnest. But the pile of writhing celebrants seemed to have little importance now.

Her daughters, tiny figures, were gazing up at the sky.

I am your mother in heaven, she thought. *But I am with you always.*

By the standards of any woman in Little Chiswick, she had lived a lifetime already. She had known married life, the raising of daughters, and widowhood. She had known relative affluence and relative poverty. Having seen her daughters settled with the best available members of the aristocracy, her life was, by all standards of those in her milieu, complete.

How blessed she was, then, to be at the beginning of another life entirely, another adventure!

Amongst the stars, *everything* was going to be an adventure, was it not? Even the most mundane of happenstances.

But first things first.

"I think, my dear," she said, "I had best make tea."

Terrestrial Passions

About the Author

Once referred to by the *International Herald Tribune* as "the most well-known expatriate Thai in the world," Somtow Sucharitkul is no longer an expatriate, since he has returned to Thailand after five decades of wandering the world. He is best known as an award-winning novelist and a composer of operas.

Born in Bangkok, Somtow grew up in Europe and was educated at Eton and Cambridge. His first career was in music and in the 1970s he acquired a reputation as a revolutionary com-poser, the first to combine Thai and Western instruments in radical new sonorities. Conditions in the arts in the region at the time proved so traumatic for the young composer that he suffered a major burnout, emigrated to the United States, and reinvented himself as a novelist.

His earliest novels were in the science fiction field but he soon began to cross into other genres. In his 1984 novel Vampire Junction, he injected a new literary inventiveness into the horror genre, in the words of Robert Bloch, author of Psycho, "skillfully combining the styles of Stephen King, William Burroughs, and the author of the Revelation to John." *Vampire Junction* was voted one of the forty all-time greatest horror books by the Horror Writers' Association, joining established classics like *Frankenstein* and *Dracula*.

In the 1990s Somtow became increasingly identified as a uniquely Asian writer with novels such as the semi-auto-biographical *Jasmine Nights*. He won the World Fantasy Award, the highest accolade given in the world of fantastic literature, for his novella *The Bird Catcher*. His fifty-three books have sold about two million copies world-wide.

After becoming a Buddhist monk for a period in 2001, Somtow decided to refocus his attention on the country of his birth, founding Bangkok's first international opera company and returning to music, where he again reinvented himself, this time as a neo-Asian neo-Romantic composer. The Norwegian government commissioned his song cycle *Songs Before Dawn* for the 100th Anniversary of the Nobel Peace Prize, and he composed at the request of the government of Thailand his *Requiem: In Memoriam 9/11* which was dedicated to the victims of the 9/11 tragedy.

According to London's Opera magazine, "in just five years, Somtow has made Bangkok into the operatic hub of Southeast Asia." His operas on Thai themes, *Madana, Mae Naak,* and *Ayodhya,* have been well received by international critics. His most recent opera, *The Silent Prince,* was premiered in 2010 in Houston, and a fifth opera, *Dan no Ura,* premiered in Thailand in the 2013 season. Since then, he has composed five more operas, and is embarking on a ten opera cycle, *DasJati - Ten Lives of the Buddha,* which if completed will be the "biggest" single work in the history of performing arts.

He is increasingly in demand as a conductor specializing in opera and in the late-romantic composers like Mahler. His repertoire runs the entire gamut from Monteverdi to Wagner. His work has been especially lauded for its stylistic authenticity and its lyricism. The orchestra he founded in Bangkok, the Siam Philharmonic, has mounted the first complete Mahler cycle in the region.

He is the first recipient of Thailand's "Distinguished Silpathorn" award, given for an artist who has made and continues to make a major impact on the region's culture, from Thailand's Ministry of Culture.

Recently, the Europa KulturForum awarded Somtow the European Cultural Achievement Award, the first Asian and only the second composer ever to receive the award.

In 2024, the Thai Government elevated Somtow to the position of National Artist, the nation's highest artistic honour.

Terrestrial Passions

By S.P. Somtow

General Fiction
The Shattered Horse
Jasmine Nights
Forgetting Places
The Other City of Angels (Bluebeard's Castle)
The Stone Buddha's Tears
Delicatus
Imperatrix

Children's Books
Dinosaur Symphony
Dinosaur Ballet
Dinosaur Opera

Dark Fantasy
The Timmy Valentine Series:
    Vampire Junction
    Valentine
    Vanitas
Vampire Junction Special Edition
Moon Dance
Darker Angels
The Vampire's Beautiful Daughter

Science Fiction
Starship & Haiku
Mallworld
The Ultimate Mallworld

The Ultimate, Ultimate, Ultimate Mallworld
Chronicles of the High Inquest:
> *Light on the Sound*
> *The Darkling Wind*
> *The Throne of Madness*
> *Utopia Hunters*
Chroniques de l'Inquisition - Volume 1 (omnibus)
Chroniques de l'Inquisition - Volume 2 (omnibus)

The Aquiliad Series:
> *Aquila in the New World*
> *Aquila and the Iron Horse*
> *Aquila and the Sphinx*

Fantasy
The Riverrun Trilogy:
> *Riverrun*
> *Armorica*
> *Yestern*
The Riverrun Trilogy (omnibus)
The Fallen Country
Wizard's Apprentice
The Snow Dragon (omnibus)

Media Tie-in
The Alien Swordmaster
Symphony of Terror
The Crow - Temple of Night
Star Trek: Do Comets Dream?

Chapbooks
Fiddling for Waterbuffaloes
I Wake from a Dream of a Drowned Star City
A Lap Dance with the Lobster Lady
Compassion — Two Perspectives
The Bird Catcher

Libretti
Mae Naak
Ayodhya
Madana
The Silent Prince
Dan no Ura
Helena Citronova
The Snow Dragon
Sama - The Faithful Son
Nemiraj - The Chariot of Heaven
Mahosadha - The Architect of Dreams

Collections
My Cold Mad Father (in press)
Fire from the Wine Dark Sea
Chui Chai (Thai)
Nova (Thai)
The Pavilion of Frozen Women
Dragon's Fin Soup
Tagging the Moon
Face of Death (Thai)
Other Edens
S.P. Somtow's The Great Tales (Thai)
Terror Nova (in press)
Terror Antiqua (in press)

Essays, Poetry and Miscellanies
Opus Fifty
A Certain Slant of "I" (in press)
Sonnets about Serial Killers
Opera East
Victory in Vienna (ed.)
Three Continents (ed.)
Nirvana Express
Caravaggio x 2
The Maestro's Noctuary
Nox
Opus One Hundred